Applause for *Skyla Hills:*

MW00940241

"When I was a l.
ing *Skylar Robbins: The Mystery of Shadow Hills*, I think Skylar is the perfect girl detective to take Nancy's place in the 21st Century. I found this book to be fun, exciting, suspenseful, and filled with adventure and great characters. I especially liked Skylar. Throughout the book, she shows a lot of character, courage and growth in some trying, scary and sticky situations. I know all Middle Grade and tween girls will totally enjoy Skylar's escapades."
— Malia Ann Haberman, author of *Chase Thinker and the House of Magic, Chase Tinker and the House of Secrets,* and *Chase Tinker and the House of Destiny*

"This book, though meant for a younger audience, kept me wanting to read more. There was mystery, suspense and a slew of relatable characters. The plot twists and ending were unexpected and exciting. It is a great choice for young adult readers."
— Kristen Mott, author of *Odie the Stray Kitten*, winner of The Next Generation Indie Book Award, and *Odie's Best Friend*

"Great MG read! I found Skylar's adventure a page-turner and I'm curious what Skylar will be up to in her next adventure."
— Bree Wolf, author of *Fireflies*

"*Skylar Robbins: The Mystery of Shadow Hills* is

the kind of novel I loved to read as a preteen girl. The curious objects involved in the story are items any girl should find interesting. The author deserves four stars for the ethnic diversity portrayed by the characters and Skylar: an imperfect girl who is observant, thinks things through, and takes action."
— N.M. Watkins, author of *Jeep O'Shea: Adventures in Time*

"Cool characters; a totally fun book. Skylar Robbins is the type of brave and inventive girl you wish you could introduce to your daughter."
— Rachel Coyne, author of *Daughter, Have I Told You?*

Skylar Robbins
The MYSTERY of the HIDDEN JEWELS

Carrie Cross

TEEN
MYSTERY
PRESS

Skylar Robbins: The Mystery of the Hidden Jewels
by Carrie Cross

ISBN:
978-0-9894143-2-6 (print)
978-0-9894143-3-3 (ebook)

Library of Congress Control Number: 2014954639

Published by Teen Mystery Press
Westlake Village, CA

Cover design: Ed Ward
www.mental-ward.com

For my dad

ACKNOWLEDGEMENTS

A huge thank you to Skylar Robbins fans and her secret agents. At the end of my first novel, *Skylar Robbins: The Mystery of Shadow Hills*, Skylar recruited agents to help solve her next case. Several of them are taking part in this interactive story by helping decode the clues Skylar shares on her website: www.skylarrobbins.com. Prospective agents can sign up and dive into this dangerous new adventure with Skylar Robbins and her BFF, Alexa. Just fill out the Secret Agent Application Form (S.A.A.F.) on the website to get your code name and Identikit.

Skylar would like to personally thank the following secret agents for their assistance in finding the hidden jewels: Kelsey G: Dragon Fire, Edmond W: Shining Onyx, Kalyn M: Hidden Shadow, Miriam W: Water Nymph, Madison R: Hunting Lion, Jared W: Thunder Cloud, Destiny M: Star Dancer, Nathanya W: Fire Princess, Samuel W: Roaring River, and Ella M: Sea Princess.

And a heartfelt thank you also goes out to Elayne Angel, Jim Cross, and Ed Ward for their excellent editorial advice and creative input.

Contents

Skylar Robbins
The MYSTERY of the HIDDEN JEWELS

1
Xandra Collins Mysteriously Disappeared

I didn't know this when I climbed into the backseat of the black Cadillac, but what was about to happen in the next half hour would change my life forever. And I'm not talking about a little change, either. This one was a monster. It wasn't just that we were moving out of the house I'd lived in since I was born, or that I was finally about to start middle school. Both of those things were huge, but they seemed like tiny details compared to what came next. The mystery I got tangled up in involved the disappearance of a famous heiress, a million dollars' worth of hidden jewels, and a threatening gang of bikers who were determined to find them before I did.

Could a skinny thirteen-year-old detective beat them to it?

You bet I could.

Well, I really hoped I could. I was so glad my BFF Alexa had my back, because I was in much more danger than I realized. Going to a new school turned out to be almost as perilous as hunting for the hidden jewels. By the time this case was solved, I'd challenged the biggest bully in the entire seventh grade, kissed my first boy, and news of my detective agency had gone viral. Not to mention I risked my life to solve a mystery.

Again.

It all started when my parents decided they wanted to buy a bigger house. They were standing in the driveway of a home we'd just looked at, talking with a woman named Victoria Knight while I sat in the car. My dad's over six feet tall, but in her high heels Ms. Knight stood eye-to-eye with him, looking like a fashion model. Her jet-black hair was pinned up in a shiny twist, and her pointy hipbones poked forward from under her slinky skirt. I pretended to read something on my iPad while I leaned toward the open window and eavesdropped.

"This next house is a classic. It was built in 1908." Ms. Knight was a realtor trying hard to sell us a house, and my parents thought that the one she just showed us had stunk.

My mom made a note on her clipboard and shook wavy brown hair away from her pretty face. She has a "widow's peak," which I think is a pretty gross name for that little point her hairline comes to in the middle of her forehead. My mom has high cheekbones and a narrow chin, so her face reminds me of a heart. Right now that heart was frowning. "That's *really* old," she commented.

"That just makes it better," my dad said. He *loves* old. "A fixer-upper is fine with me. We'll remodel," he suggested, looking at my mom with his hands spread wide.

"It's got six bedrooms, five baths, a ballroom, a library, and more!" Ms. Knight exclaimed.

My mom's forehead continued to wrinkle. "Six bedrooms when there's only Skylar and us? Isn't that overkill?" she asked, glancing at the realtor.

My dad pushed his glasses up the bridge of his nose and considered this. "So, it's big. I like big. And it's in the same school district as our current house, so Skylar can still go to Pacific Middle School with her friends."

Yes! I thought, squeezing my iPad while I waited for my mom's reply. It was as if my dad had read my mind: like he knew I couldn't wait to get to Pacific to see all my friends again, and Dustin Coles: the smartest, cutest, most popular boy going into seventh grade.

"That's very important to girls her age," the realtor said.

It sure is. Score one for you, Ms. Knight. I peeked out the window and noticed she had a weird look on her face. Like she wasn't telling us everything. After the dangerous summer I'd just spent in Shadow Hills, my radar was on high alert for liars.

My mom frowned. "But the place is so old it must be falling apart."

"It's not—falling apart," Ms. Knight said.

"Samantha. *1908.*" My dad rolled the date off his tongue as if it tasted good. "Let's give it a shot, Honey. I'll bet it has a heck of a history."

Ms. Knight's cheeks turned pink. She made her shiny maroon lips into a circle and blew out a slow breath. Then she scratched at a spot on the pavement with the toe of her high-heeled shoe. "Oh, the house has a history, that's for sure."

I'll bet it does, I thought, opening the note-taking app and jotting down some ideas on my iPad:

Ms. K is worried abt nxt house. Posing. Won't look m & d in the eye.

I watched her for a minute and added another note:

? wrong w/ nxt house?

My mom obviously hadn't noticed Ms. Knight's strange reaction, because when she looked at my dad,

3

she smiled. She was an American history professor at UCLA and loved anything "with a history". My dad loved anything classic, antique, or just plain old. He's a chemist and an inventor, but with his short, light brown hair and his wire-rimmed glasses my dad looked like he could be a college professor himself.

No one would suspect the laboratory he worked in looked like a mad scientist's and that he'd almost blown off his eyebrows when I was in first grade. Faint pink scars still speckle his forehead from when one of his concoctions exploded. If he hadn't been wearing his goggles he could have ended up blind. Whenever I want permission to do something my mom thinks is dangerous she brings up my dad's accident and asks me if I want to "follow in the risk-taker's footsteps," or "think it through more carefully first," like she would.

I usually end up taking the risks.

After finishing my detective notes I looked out the window trying to catch my mom's eye, hoping they'd hurry up and get in the car so we could get this over with. I didn't want to move in the first place.

The house I grew up in is in Santa Monica, real close to the beach. I've investigated every square inch of our neighborhood, and I know its woodsy streets by heart. My best friend Alexa O'Reilly lives right around the corner. We've been BFFs since second grade when she moved here from Texas. She still has a tiny bit of a Southern accent. Like she calls cement, "*SEA*-ment." Then I'll say, "Sea-ment?" and Alexa's green eyes look surprised. Then her freckled cheeks will bunch up and she'll laugh at herself.

I've never had a friend as good as Alexa. Her excitement always makes everything fun and she cracks me up. This summer I got stuck at my cousin Gwendolyn's house in Malibu for eight weeks while my parents toured Europe. That's when I realized the meaning of true friendship. I went to summer school in Shadow Hills, and met a girl in art class named Kat who claimed to be a witch. She passed me notes in backward writing and thought up all these cool art projects we could do together. After casting dangerous spells with Kat in an abandoned garden and getting to know her better, I wondered if she just liked to trick everyone for her own benefit. Hanging out with Kat made me realize what a good friend Alexa really was. What real friends would do *for* each other, and wouldn't do *to* each other.

When my parents got back from Europe they had huge news. My dad finally sold the formula for a non-alcoholic cough syrup he'd invented, and while they were in Paris a major drug company paid him a huge fee. Suddenly we were in the market for a much bigger house, and my mom couldn't wait to move out of our small one. I didn't care that we suddenly had more money than we used to have. The only thing that mattered to me was that my family was about to move. If my parents buy a home very far away, Alexa and I won't be able to go to the same middle school, and we've been looking forward to going to Pacific together forever.

My mom climbed into the backseat beside me and I quietly closed the cover on my iPad. Ms. Knight turned around and gave us a big smile. "I'm excited about the next house." She sounded like she was acting. "I can't wait to see how you like it," she told my dad. He was sitting next to her in front because he was too tall for the back seat. We drove for a couple of blocks and I watched the ocean while we waited for the light to turn green so we could turn onto Pacific Coast Highway.

The white water rushing toward the sand churned messily, like each swirling bit couldn't decide in which direction to go. The dark blue water near the horizon looked calm, but between the deep water and the shore there was a threatening, shifting movement. It made me nervous. Like something was welling up and heading toward us. Something dangerous that couldn't be stopped. One wave after another loomed slowly in the distance, rising higher and building power before rolling steadily forward. Then each one crashed down onto the sand, exploding into bubbly white froth.

We'd lived a few minutes away from the Santa Monica pier since I was born, so I know its roller coaster and game booths like I know my backyard. Looking out the window, I imagined the smell of buttered popcorn and corndogs as we drove up the coast with the windows rolled up. I remembered how good it felt to ride the Ferris wheel, like I was soaring over the sea. My favorite car was the pink one. I didn't mind its rusty sides or the cracked leather seat. When you rode that Ferris wheel up into the sky and looked out over the sparkling ocean it felt like you were on top of the world.

"We're not going to move far from here, are we?" I asked my mom for the tenth time. "I'll die if I can't go to Pacific with Alexa." *Not to mention Dustin*, I thought, but didn't say. Dustin Coles was president of student council, got almost straight A's, and his huge hazel eyes and dimples were off the charts. I'd only admitted this to Alexa and to my own diary, but I'd been crushing on him for two years. And over the summer something amazing happened: Alexa told me that while I was away she saw Dustin at a party I'd missed. She said it like she was about to spill a delicious secret.

And then she did.

"He asked where you were."

"He did? *No way." I snuggled into the cushion, eager to hear more.*

"Swear. I told him you went to summer school in Malibu and he thought that was really cool."

"He really said that? Did he say, 'that's cool,' or, 'that's really cool'?"

Alexa laughed. "I'm pretty sure he said, 'Malibu? Wow. That's cool.'"

"Awesome," I said, hugging my pillow and smiling.

Why had Dustin asked where I was? Was he just curious why I wasn't with Alexa as usual? Or maybe he was worried that I was off having fun with some other guy. Wondering if I'd met a cute surfer in Malibu and had forgotten all about him. *I wished he was worrying about me.* Then I came to my senses. As if I could actually make Dustin Coles jealous, right? But he *did* ask about me. That had to mean something.

If I couldn't go to Pacific Middle School with Dustin, Alexa, and all of my other friends, it would absolutely destroy me. Not to mention what it would do to my BFF. She's carrying around a big, embarrassing secret. And I'm trying to help her keep it.

My mom grabbed my hand and squeezed it. "We'll have to see which house is the best fit for us, Sweetheart. It may be in a different neighborhood. If it is, you'll adapt, and we'll come back and visit the pier." This made my stomach knot up.

A few black-bellied clouds edged across the mountains toward us. Their reflections were the color of pencil lead on the green-blue part of the water. Then the wind kicked up, and the treetops on the hillside started to dance. "Rain's coming," my dad said, squinting up at the sky.

"There's supposed to be an unusually strong summer storm on its way," Ms. Knight agreed, her dark eyes catching mine in the rearview mirror. "Hopefully we'll make it to the top of the hill before it hits." She glanced at my dad. "This house is the last one in the area that is in your price range, and it's quite a bargain, considering the breathtaking views and its size."

I didn't care how big our next house was, I just didn't want to move far away from Alexa. Our house had already sold, so we needed to find a new one to move into very soon. We had looked at homes all day last Saturday and Sunday and I was sick of it.

"So what else can you tell us about the house?" my mom asked.

"Well, the woman who owned it was *Xandra Collins*." Victoria Knight said the name like she was letting us in on a juicy secret. She pronounced it *Zandra*, not *EX-an-dra*.

"Why does her name sound familiar? Did I read about her somewhere?" my dad asked.

"I'm sure you saw stories about her in the tabloids."

My mom let out a little snort and smiled. "We don't read gossip magazines."

Victoria Knight raised one eyebrow. "Well she was all over the regular news too. The Collins family was rich. *Really* rich. When her parents died, Xandra Collins inherited millions. *Many* millions. She gave tons of money to various charities. That's one of the reasons she kept making the news. Xandra Collins was wealthy and beautiful, but also quite—unusual." She looked sideways at my dad. "Three years ago she mysteriously disappeared. Her mansion has been vacant ever since."

"What happened to her?" I leaned toward the front seat, eager to hear more.

"Skylar," my mother warned.

"What? I'm just curious." I'm going to become an undercover detective like my grandfather, so I love anything mysterious. I looked out the window as a jagged bolt of lightning streaked across the windshield and lit up the gloomy sky. Moments later, thunder boomed above us like an exploding cannon. Ms. Knight didn't answer my question.

"Xandra Collins's jewelry collection was legendary too. Every magazine showed her dripping in diamonds. The house is incredible. Wait 'til you see it."

"I definitely remember hearing about her," my father said as we turned off Pacific Coast Highway and headed up into Santa Monica Canyon.

"I'm sure you did. There was quite a scandal concerning her disappearance." Ms. Knight steered onto a winding street that was so narrow we had to pull partway into someone's driveway so a car on the other side could get around us. The wind gusted and a bunch of dead leaves splatted against the windshield. She edged carefully back onto the road.

"What was the scandal about?" I asked, my fingers on my iPad, ready to take notes.

"It doesn't matter," my father said, turning around to look at me. My dad has light blue eyes that crinkle around the edges when he smiles. But right now he wasn't smiling.

"I don't remember all the details." Ms. Knight played with her earring as she glanced at my dad again. I could tell this was a lie. She definitely remembered the details. But for some reason she didn't want to give them up.

"Oh, go ahead and tell her," he said. "She'll figure it out anyway."

Ms. Knight took a deep breath. "Rumor was, Xandra Collins was being stalked. Then she disappeared without a trace. So people thought maybe…someone killed her."

My mom started flicking the metal clamp on her clipboard. *Someone murdered the woman whose house we might buy?* She didn't like the sound of that at all. Ms. Knight looked at her in the rearview mirror. "But it might not be true. They never found her body."

"I'll bet she was kidnapped," I suggested.

My dad looked over his shoulder and smiled. "Maybe she ran off with a mystery man," he said, wiggling his eyebrows.

"Maybe she went on a secret cruise around the world looking for more diamonds," I suggested, "Or—"

My mom laughed. "All right, you two."

Tapping my iPad, I continued my notes, hoping my mom wouldn't look over and read them.

3 yrs ago X.C. disappeared, "without a trace." *Everyone* **leaves a trace.**

"Xandra Collins's heirs finally stopped fighting over the house and decided to sell it," Ms. Knight continued. "The place just went on the market this morning so I haven't had a chance to preview it yet. I think it may need some work since it's been vacant for three years," she admitted.

A fistful of raindrops hit the windshield. "Are we almost there?" I asked.

"Just about," Ms. Knight said. Right after that it started to pour. She took her eyes off the road for a second to glance at the address while the rain drummed on the roof of the car.

"Careful!" my mother warned as we swerved around a wet bend. She grabbed the door with one hand and the front seat with the other. Her clipboard slid off her lap onto the seat between us. I looked down the side of the hill and realized how high up we'd climbed. Now the ocean looked like a cold, gray sheet of steel as it reflected the cloud-filled sky.

The street ended in a cul-de-sac. This was good. I remembered something Grandpa used to say: *Criminals don't bother with houses in cul-de-sacs. They don't want to get trapped with no way out.* I found out later that not every criminal knew the rule about cul-de-sacs. Ms. Knight steered up a driveway that curved into the hill and I stared at the house that loomed above us, perched on the edge of the hillside like it was growing there. A steel gate with pointed spikes guarded the house, as if it were warning us to keep out. Or maybe it was keeping something in.

"Well folks, we're here."

Framed in the wet windshield, dark storm clouds hung over the abandoned mansion, their bottoms bulging like they were about to burst. The front of the house was covered in multi-colored stone. Behind cracked windows and torn screens, tattered curtains fluttered into the house, billowing inside on the damp breeze. The roof had several different levels and was missing a bunch of shingles. A round tower with a tip like an upside-down ice-cream cone stretched up the front of the mansion, pointing at the sky. Ms. Knight called it a *turret*, and sounded like she was proud the place had one. There was a tiny room at the top of the turret that was higher than any other part of the house. It seemed to be calling my name. *Skylar Robbins*, it whispered. *Come explore.*

We got out of the car into the wind and rain and hurried toward the house. Crumbling stepping-stones led us through a lawn that was overgrown with knee-high weeds. Dead trees sported black branches that ended in grasping claws. As Victoria Knight fumbled with the key, I saw that the curtains were stained with something that looked like blood.

"Here we go," she said, opening the tall front door. She let out a loud shriek and ducked.

2
Find the Dumbwaiter

A big gray pigeon flew out of the house, its wings flapping right past her face. Recovering quickly, she stepped inside and held the door open for us. "It's been closed up for a long time. I had no idea there would be—oh!" Another frightened bird escaped from the deserted mansion and Ms. Knight's hand flew up to protect her hairdo.

"That's OK." My dad put his hand on my back and ushered me into the dim entryway. A broken mirror decorated with gold veins and spider webs hung on the wall and I looked into it. My dark, straight hair was messy from the wind and my blue eyes were round with excitement.

"Can we turn on the lights, or is the power dead?" my mom asked, rubbing her arms like she was trying to get rid of the cold.

Ms. Knight flipped a switch, but nothing happened. "The electricity must have been turned off when Xandra disappeared and stopped paying her utility bills. If you'd rather see it on a sunnier—"

"No," I surprised everyone by saying loudly. I looked at my parents. "Can we please see the rest of the house?" My dad nodded, and we followed the realtor out of the entryway and into the living room.

"Oh, it's so dirty," my mom complained, holding up a corner of a curtain that had some brownish stains on it.

"Is that blood?" I asked, aiming my iPad and taking a

quick picture.

"Bird doo," my mom said, letting go of the curtain.

Trailing vines had grown through the busted windows and taken root in the soiled carpet. Like the outside wanted to grow its way in, and it had in a big way. Ugly tan roots with knobs and boils slithered through cracks in the windows, crept down the walls, and burrowed through the carpet and into the floor. Then the roots spread, sending tentacles in every direction. It looked like a giant, gray-green octopus had taken over the living room.

"I know it needs some updating, but with a fresh coat of paint and a woman's touch," Ms. Knight hinted, smiling at my mother, "this place will have real charm. Let's look at the rest of this floor at least, shall we?"

"Sure, let's explore a little more of the house. We drove all the way up here," my father said, smiling gently at my mom.

Excellent, I thought. *He likes it too.*

As Ms. Knight led us out of the living room she described the house. "It has at least three floors."

"At least three?" My father smiled. "You aren't sure?"

"It looks to me like it's got three, but the listing agent said there are four. She probably meant the attic or the little room at the top of the turret."

When no one was looking I typed a detective note:
There may be a hidden floor.

We followed Ms. Knight into a larger room that she called, "the ballroom." There were mirrors on some walls and broken windows on the others. It had high ceilings with designs stamped into the plaster, and it smelled awful. Rain leaked in through the cracked glass, and below the windowsills soggy patches of carpet stunk up the room. It smelled old and moldy and damp and rotten, like really bad breath. My dad looked around the ballroom with an intense look on his face, nodding to himself.

"This house has *character*," Ms. Knight said as she led us down a pitch-black hall toward the long kitchen. A little light came in through small windows and I noticed that lots of the kitchen drawers were pulled out. All of them were empty, and a few were upside down on the floor, scattered between piles of what my dad called, "rat dirt." Someone had really searched this place thoroughly. I wondered what they had been looking for.

A round cast-iron stove sat in one corner, and the rest of the kitchen looked just as old-fashioned. There was a weird telephone with a separate earpiece and a crank attached to the wall next to some wood shelves. "Will you look at that antique," my dad said, walking over to it. "Never thought I'd see one of these." I figured it probably didn't work anymore, but it would be fun to use if it did.

My mom leaned against the counter and looked around the kitchen. "Ugh!" she cried suddenly. Her hand had landed in a pile of something white and brown and gooey that a pigeon had left behind. She looked at it, and then groaned as she showed me her palm, trying not to laugh. When she turned the handle on the sink, nothing came out of the faucet.

"Sorry. Here's a tissue." The realtor handed my mom a Kleenex, then turned to smile at my dad and me. "There's something else you should know about the house. After

Xandra Collins was presumed dead, the heirs divided her belongings but they couldn't find her jewelry box. At first they assumed the box was stolen, but then they found a mysterious note, written in her handwriting," Ms. Knight said.

My ears pricked up like a German shepherd's. "What kind of mysterious note?"

"The note said she had hidden her jewelry box somewhere on the estate. And whoever is smart and brave enough to follow the clues she left behind will be rewarded by inheriting her fortune in diamonds."

"Wow," I said, trying to memorize the wording of the note. "It almost sounds like she knew she was going to disappear beforehand." All three of them looked at me with their eyebrows shooting up. They were probably surprised that I'd thought of it before any of the adults did. "What clues did she leave?" I asked Ms. Knight as we followed her out of the kitchen.

"That's the thing. Her heirs searched the whole house, but they couldn't turn up any clues." She made a sad face at me, like it was too bad that the clues didn't exist.

But I thought this was great. I couldn't wait to break out my detective kit and start looking for the clues. Xandra's heirs just weren't smart enough to find them.

This meant the jewelry box was still hidden.

"Now, in addition to the large rooms on all of the floors," Ms. Knight continued.

"All three or four of them," my dad joked.

"There's a dumbwaiter, a butler's pantry, a gazebo, and a greenhouse."

"A dumbwaiter? Like in *Harriet the Spy?*" I asked.

16

Ms. Knight ignored me, leading us into a little room behind the kitchen. "This is the butler's pantry." There were many shelves for storing food, a deep metal sink, and a second dishwasher. "Just look at all this cupboard space!" She smiled at my mom and waved her arm through the air. "You have a ton of storage."

"Is this where the dumb waiter works?" I joked, and my dad put his hand on my shoulder.

"Show us the dumbwaiter, please," he said to Ms. Knight.

She looked embarrassed. "Actually, I don't know exactly where it is." At the end of the butler's pantry there was a narrow door. Ms. Knight jiggled the handle but it was locked. "A dumbwaiter is like a small elevator—too small for a person to ride," she explained. "The cook could set meals in it to be carried up to the master bedroom or to the formal dining room on the second floor. Some homeowners use dumbwaiters to lift books up to the library or carry heavy items to the top floors of their houses."

"Thank you," I said as my fingers tapped my iPad.

Find the dumbwaiter.

"In addition to the living room and ballroom, there is a sitting room, a study, and a library. Over twenty rooms in all."

That's a lot of places to search for clues, I thought.

We walked up the first flight of stairs and I wandered into a bedroom and looked out the window. From this high up, all I could see were the ragged mountaintops across the canyon and an occasional flash of lightning. Looking down, I noticed that a black metal railing ran around the edge of the side yard, surrounding the property like a rodeo ring. It was about four feet high and had upright posts about every four inches. One part was dented badly into a big *V*, like it had been bashed in or struck by lightning. I would have to be careful if I explored outside at night. If I stumbled through that part of the railing in the dark I could plunge down the rocky hillside and disappear like Xandra Collins.

After touring the second floor and then the third, I lost count of the rooms and couldn't remember my way back to the front door. My dad liked the house, and I craved it. I just had to live here. "Could I have that little round room in the turret for my bedroom?" I asked. "The one on the third floor—or the fourth. Depending on how many there really are." My dad didn't answer, but he did give me a wink.

The room I wanted was very small, but it had a spiral staircase on one side that led up to the tip of the turret, where there was a cozy round room that I loved. It would be perfect for my detective office. Its ceiling came to a point, it had windows all around, and it was so high up that you could see in every direction for miles. Since it was the end of summer, the mountains were covered with dry grass and brush that had browned in the sun. Way past the tips of those mountains I saw the blue-green sea shimmering in the distance. It was my favorite thing in the entire world: the ocean surging powerfully forward, vast and beautiful. Plus, if we bought this house I'd still live pretty close to all of my friends, and I'd get to go to Pacific with Alexa and Dustin.

"I'll have to show you the backyard another time

because of the rain, but how do you like it so far?" Ms. Knight asked my mom.

"We'll need a gardener to rip all those vines out of the living room before we can even think about remodeling." My mother looked like she smelled something unpleasant. "The whole house is really grimy and in pretty poor shape." She probably thought it was grimy because her hand had landed in bird poop.

"I'll clean it," I offered.

"It does need an awful lot of work," my father said, looking around.

"I'll help," I pleaded. "I'll weed the carpet."

"It's quite a bargain," Ms. Knight said. "It won't last."

"Can we get it?" I begged my dad.

He looked at my mother and smiled, crinkling his eyes. I could tell he liked it too.

"We'll think about it," my mom answered.

3
Abandoned Mansion

Even though they hadn't decided which house to buy, my mom told me I'd better not wait until the last minute to pack. She suggested I go through my cupboards and make bags of toys to give to the homeless shelter. I figured the sooner I packed, the faster she'd have to make up her mind about the mansion on the hill. She couldn't let me sit around in an empty room, right? So the next morning I took my creative writing notebooks and my journal out of a desk drawer and piled them in a box with my art supplies. I cleaned out the drawer in my bedside stand, packing several old notepads, a candle, and some favorite rocks and seashells I'd picked up on the beach. Using a thick black marker I labeled this box, "Skylar–personal and private."

Then I packed my book collection. I had so many favorites it took three boxes to hold them all. Picking out a bunch of games and toys I'd outgrown, I put them in another box and marked it, "Donate." Looking out my bedroom window, I saw the tree house my dad built, my swing set, and mom's garden. Our backyard, our house, our neighborhood. Everything I'd grown up with was about to change.

I pictured the warped board in the middle of my tree house floor. I always had to be careful not to trip over it on the short walk to the other side of the "dining room." This was where I liked to eat my afternoon snack while watching the neighborhood through the pink Super-

20

Zoom binoculars my grandpa gave me for my birthday. Leaning out the window eating peanut butter crackers, I'd look up and down my block hoping to see something mysterious. Or maybe some cute boys playing ball in the park down the street. Staring into the backyard, I realized I'd better spend as many afternoons in the tree house as possible while I still had the chance.

Then I thought about another dining room: the one we ate in on Sunday nights when my grandfather came over for dinner. My mom called it, "the formal dining room." That cracked me up since it was smaller and more cramped than where we usually ate, but when Grandpa came over, out came the linen tablecloth and the silver that needed that smelly gray polish to clean.

Not that my dad's father wanted anything fancy. Not even. Grandpa used to joke that he was "nothin' but a street cop," and then his blue eyes would crinkle around the edges like my dad's. His favorite part of dinner was dessert, just like me. Sometimes he'd sneak us a couple of Oreos before dinner, and when I was younger we'd pretend we were in a commercial together. We'd twist off the tops, look at each other while we quickly dunked our cookies in the same glass of milk, and then we'd stuff them in our mouths while we laughed.

My grandfather always made everything fun. I remembered going to my favorite seafood restaurant with him when I was six years old.

"Don't worry, I'll keep Skylar busy," Grandpa said, winking at my mom as we followed the hostess to our table.

Goody! We got a window seat. Waves crashed right next to us on the other side of the glass, spraying white foam into the air like someone had just turned on a gigantic fountain. It was exciting and I talked too loud. "Use your restaurant voice please," my mom said.

Grandpa held up one finger, catching my attention. "Let's play Silent Detective," he whispered.

I nodded fast, wiggling in my seat.

"I see something…blue." My grandfather's merry smile and folded arms challenged me to figure out what it was. If I said anything out loud, I would lose. After looking around the restaurant for a second, I pointed out the window at the ocean.

I raised my eyebrows but Grandpa shook his head. Too easy. I tugged on my ear, signaling that I needed my first clue. He pointed at me with both index fingers, and then moved them closer together. Something smaller.

A lady sitting near us wore a light blue blouse. Grabbing a tuft of my shirt, I tilted my head in her direction and mouthed, "Her top?" while raising my eyebrows.

Was I right?

Grandpa blinked twice, signaling no. Brought his fingers together again. Something smaller than that.

I looked slowly around the restaurant. A big, multi-colored bouquet sat on a table near the entrance. Bright blue peacock feathers poked up in between green ferns and some weird-looking red-orange flowers. I pointed at the bouquet and flapped my arms like a bird. "Peacock feathers?" I mouthed silently.

Blink, blink. Wrong again.

I needed my second clue and tugged my ear again. If I couldn't guess it after two clues, I would lose the game. My grandfather touched his fingertips together and pulled *his hands toward his body: Silent Detective language for something closer. I concentrated on our table. Nothing on it was blue. I looked at my dad's colorful tie. No blue there either.*

A busboy set down four glasses of ice water and my mom reached for hers and took a sip. Her ring sparkled. Grinning with my success, I pointed at the blue gem on her finger and watched Grandpa touch his nose and smile. I'd won Silent Detective. "I'm proud of you," he said, reaching forward just as the waiter came to take our order. Grandpa pulled a quarter out of my ear, and I got to keep the prize.

My eyes started to sting like they always did when I was trying not to cry. I missed my grandfather, and I was going to miss my tree house.

There wasn't much packing left to do so I got back to it. In a far corner of my bedside drawer, my fingers touched a flat white box. I'd slept with it beside me for three years. The item inside meant more to me than anything else I owned, so there was no way I was going to risk misplacing it by packing it in a carton. Picking it up off the fluffy cotton pad, I wrapped the oval in tissue and zipped it into the secret compartment in my purse where I knew it would be safe.

When my nightstand was empty except for my cherry Chapstick, I took a break and grabbed my iPhone. It was a hand-me-down from when my dad got the latest model. He gave his old one to my mom, and I got hers. A crack sliced the screen and it needed a new cover, but it worked and that was all I cared about. I called Alexa. "You will not believe this awesome house we may be getting." I sat on my bed and hugged my knees, fantasizing about moving into the small bedroom in the turret.

"Will you still get to go to Pacific?" If we didn't start seventh grade together it would destroy us both. But it would be way worse for her.

"If we buy this house. It's in Santa Monica Canyon, not far from here. Just up a really steep hill."

"I won't be able to take it if you have to go to a different middle school," Alexa said, and I knew how much she meant it.

"Me too. My mom said if we get this house I'll still go to Pacific."

"I *hope*." I pictured Alexa shaking thick strawberry blonde curls away from her pretty face and smiling in relief. "Then you'll still get to see Dustin, too."

Oh, yum.

Dustin Coles is definitely the cutest boy going into seventh grade. I smiled, imagining his wavy brown hair and straight white teeth. He was the fastest runner in school, and the P.E. teachers always chose him to be team captain. Even in class Dustin always seemed to be the leader. The other boys looked up to him and the girls all tried to sit next to him. He's one of the few boys who are taller than I am, he's super nice, and he never, ever laughs at Alexa.

"I just have to convince my mom to buy this house. She's not that into it. I'll call you later. I better go." I bit the side of my thumb.

"Please talk her into it. My fingers are crossed."

"So are mine."

The following weekend we went back to the abandoned mansion with Ms. Knight. If we *had* to move, the turret house was the one for me. I just had to convince my mom.

"First of all, Mom, it's huge, it's cool, and it has a *greenhouse*." We both love to garden so I was hoping for a smiling nod, but she just raised an eyebrow at me. "More importantly," I said, trying to sound intelligent, "it's close to Pacific, and UCLA, and dad will have plenty of space to set up his gadget room." Leaving my old block was hard enough. Starting middle school with a bunch of people I didn't know would stink beyond belief. "And it's safe. Since it's in a cul-de-sac, right?" I took a deep breath and waited for my mom's reply.

She looked at me, shaking her head a little. "Being in a cul-de-sac doesn't guarantee your safety. Plus, it's dirty, it's in shambles, and it's covered in bird and rat filth," she said, glancing back and forth at my dad and me like we were nuts.

"We can get a cleaning crew in here. And replacing the curtains and repainting the walls will be affordable," my father reasoned. "That ballroom downstairs would be perfect for a home laboratory," he said slowly. "It's big enough to conduct experiments and there's plenty of room for all my—stuff." I grinned hugely. He was definitely on my side. My mom didn't look convinced. Until his next sentence. "I could work in there after hours instead of at the lab. I could be home for dinner every night." This made her smile. For a split second.

"It also needs new flooring, new appliances, new windows…." She ticked the items off on her fingers. "This isn't going to be cheap."

"We can afford it now, Honey. Remember?" my dad

reminded her.

She nodded thoughtfully, and then looked at me. "But how are you going to ride your bike up this hill?"

"I'll push it if I have to. Or maybe you can take Alexa and me to school on your way to work and her mom can take us home." I had never been so determined to get anything in my life. Getting an *A* in English or learning to do a handspring were things I could accomplish on my own. I hated having to ask someone else for something I really wanted, but I would have promised my parents anything it took to get them to buy this house. I couldn't believe it even came with a mystery and clues to hidden jewels! My detective tools would definitely come in handy.

I never imagined the amount of danger I was about to put myself in, or how much I would need Alexa by my side. Not to mention the secret agents that had joined my agency after I solved my last mystery, like agent # 009 Sea Princess and # 007 Shining Onyx. The more boys and girls I had working on clues with me the better.

Ms. Knight held up one finger. "Now if you'll follow me outside, I'll show you the backyard, the gazebo, and the greenhouse."

"Yes," my mom agreed. "Let's see the greenhouse."

I hurried to catch up, reaching for her arm and smiling. "Mom, the greenhouse can be your spot like mine is the turret room." She rolled her eyes at me, but she still looked as though she liked the idea.

We followed Ms. Knight across the weed-covered lawn and over to the greenhouse. She walked up two stairs and struggled with the rusty door handle. I peered through the dirty windows and saw a bunch of dead plants and a filthy counter with cupboards and drawers underneath it. Some of the drawers had been pulled out and were lying on the floor. She got the door open and my mom and I walked inside and looked at a grubby workbench and rusty tools hanging on hooks. The floor was made of dirty wood planks that were stained and split. The greenhouse stunk, like something had been wet for too long. I thought it was pretty gross, but my mom looked into every corner like this moldy place was amazing. When she jotted notes on her clipboard, this time she actually looked happy.

"And finally," Ms. Knight held her hand out as if she were offering something to us, "the gazebo."

"The what?" I asked.

"Ga-ZEE-bo." My mom pronounced it slowly, like I hadn't heard her.

"OK, but I still don't know what one *is*."

"Gazebos are cool little outdoor rooms. Come on, let's go look at it." She seemed excited, like we were about to explore a new store that carried all her favorite things at half price. Ms. Knight led us over to a small, six-sided structure made of white-painted wood. There were benches attached to the inside walls with faded cushions on them, and a little table sat in the middle. The roof of the gazebo ended in a point, matching the top of the turret. A bird's nest perched on one of its beams. The nest was layered with twigs and pine needles and torn pieces of dirty white paper.

"What do you do in a gazebo?" I asked.

"They're just cozy open-air rooms where you can have tea or brunch." Now my mom had a big smile on her face. "Or you can sit in here on a nice spring day and read. Of course it needs new cushions and a fresh coat of paint," she told my father, and I laughed.

My dad winked at me as I asked, "So when are we moving in?"

4
Teen Detective's Office

A few weeks later my dad pulled up to the curb in front of our new house and parked, leaving the driveway open for the moving van. I looked up at the tall stone mansion, holding my detective kit. The barren front yard was covered in dusty gravel, tall weeds, and wispy, water-starved vines. The roofline went up and down like a staircase. Or like more than one person had designed the house and they forgot to talk to each other about it before it was built.

The turret was calling my name, and I couldn't stop wondering how many floors there really were: three, or four? I congratulated myself on convincing my parents to buy this house, while they celebrated the deal they had gotten. We were all happy about how fast the sale closed, which meant we were able to move in before school started.

My mom had hired a cleaning crew, and all of the bird and rat turds and spider webs were gone. The broken windows had been replaced and we had new travertine floors. There was a lot of unpacking and organizing to do before I could start exploring, but I was so excited about moving into the mansion that I didn't even care. The only thing I was worried about was getting the bedroom I wanted with the cool spiral staircase. And the pointed room at the top of the turret for my detective agency.

One of my most cherished belongings is Grandpa's old desk. I love the slippery feel of the polished wood, and best of all it has secret compartments. The drawer in the center has a panel behind it that pulls sideways, revealing a little chamber. This is my favorite spot to hide money and my most prized possession. I thought Grandpa's desk would just fit inside that little round room.

"There are so many bigger bedrooms," my mother said. "Why would you pick the smallest one?"

My dad stuck up for me. "Hey, if I were a kid I'd want to live in that turret too. Like Rapunzel, right Skylar?" He took his microscope cases out of the trunk and gently closed the hood. He wouldn't let the moving men touch any of his equipment.

"Fairy tales have nothing to do with it, Dad." Wrapping long hair behind my ears, I looked right into my mom's eyes. "I don't care how small my bedroom is. I just want that pointy turret room above it for my *office*." It was the perfect spot for a detective to nestle in and solve a whopper of a mystery. Like where had Xandra Collins hidden her jewelry box before she disappeared?

I couldn't get Ms. Knight's words out of my mind. *She hid her jewelry box somewhere on the estate. Whoever is smart enough and brave enough to follow the clues she left behind will be rewarded by inheriting her fortune in diamonds.* And her heirs couldn't find a single clue in three years!

"You want an office to work in? That's a good reason," my mom said, turning to the movers. "The big desk goes upstairs." The one with the dark wavy hair looked at her until she gave him a nod. Then they picked up my heavy desk with their muscles bulging.

"Thanks, Mom." I carried a box of art supplies up two

30

flights of stairs with a giant pair of moving men following, and led them into my bedroom. "My desk goes up there." I pointed up the spiral staircase.

The dark-haired guy groaned, and the short blond with the freckled arms swore. If my mom had heard him say the *s*-word in front of me she would have freaked. "I'm sorry, I know it's heavy. But you guys look like you work out like—all the time." Their arms were bigger than my thighs. "You can get it up there, can't you?" I smiled hopefully.

The blond nodded his head at me. "Smart kid," he commented. "Knows how to get what she wants." They grunted and heaved, turned my heavy desk on its end, and managed to get it up the stairs and into the little room in the tip of the turret. One of them yelled, "Where do you want it facing?"

I bolted up the staircase and made a careful decision, looking out all the windows and picking the best view. "Facing that way, please." I pointed across the railing at the edge of the yard. The rocky cliffs fell away into the canyon below. Beyond the other side of the mountains I could see a slice of dark blue ocean foaming in the distance. With my desk positioned that way I could look out over the canyon and watch the sun set or a storm rage while I was at my desk doing homework or working on the mystery of the hidden jewels.

After the movers positioned my desk, I followed them back to their truck and got a big box containing a multicolored stained-glass lamp I'd bought for four dollars at a garage sale. It had a brass base and dangly crystals hanging all around the edge of the shade. A few of the crystals were missing, but I just thought it made the lamp seem more antique, like something you'd find in the library inside an old castle. Which is exactly how I wanted to decorate my office.

Then I unzipped the pocket in my purse and took out the item I'd carefully wrapped in tissue. The gold shield had an eagle curled around the top, and DET. ROBBINS was stamped across the badge in block letters. I remembered when I'd gotten it. It was a horrible day, and I wasn't ready.

"Skylar, always remember to look for clues in unexpected places. They won't be sitting right under your nose, waiting for you to find them." Grandpa's papery fingers touched my arm and he pulled me closer to him on the hospital bed. I could tell by the look on his face that he was about to say something important. "I want you to have this." My grandfather pressed his detective badge into my hand and folded my fingers around it. "Skylar, don't ever let anyone tell you there is something you cannot do. There is no mystery or problem you cannot solve, and nothing you can't achieve if you set your mind to it."

It was the best advice I'd ever gotten, and some of the last words my grandfather ever spoke to me. I pictured his face as I turned the golden oval over in my hand and ran my fingers over its shiny surface. Then I set his badge on the cotton pad and closed the little white box.

My grandfather left me his beautiful wood desk in his will. Opening the center drawer, I slid the top drawer completely out and opened the chamber hiding behind it, slipping the box into the hidden compartment. Working on mysteries at Grandpa's desk with his badge inside would be inspiring, like he was close by. Thinking about it made me feel like a real detective.

I topped the antique desk with orange-, mint-, and chocolate-scented candles and a small fern in a clay pot, and then walked down the stairs to my bedroom. I wanted to hurry and finish unpacking so I could start to explore our new house and the yard. After my grandfather figured something out, he used to dust off his hands with satisfaction and say, "Case *closed*." Even though he was gone, I wanted to close my own case and feel like I'd made him proud of me. And there were clues hidden somewhere in this house just waiting for me to find them.

5
Nerves

The day before school started I went over to Alexa's and her mom gave us a ride to the drugstore. "I'm so glad your parents bought the turret house," Alexa said as we walked inside. "That would completely reek if you had to go to a different school."

"I know, right?" I agreed, looking around the crowded store. "I can't believe tomorrow is—"

"Middle school!" Alexa grabbed my arm. She was even more nervous than I was. We walked down the wide center aisle, heading for the makeup department.

"Have you been practicing sign language?" I asked. A hearing-impaired boy in my summer school class had taught me some signs, and I'd loved watching the interpreter translate during class. I taught myself the fingerspelling alphabet from a chart I found online:

When I got back from Shadow Hills I watched sign language videos on YouTube, and then taught the signs to Alexa so we could tell secrets in school and no one would know what we were talking about.

She nodded, bouncing her fist twice. YES

I touched my lips with my right hand, and then lowered the back of that hand into my left palm. GOOD

Alexa looked at me and tried to fingerspell S-E-C-R-T L-A-N-G-U-G. I figured out that she meant *secret language*, and we both smiled.

I love the stationery aisle, and we spent a long time in it debating over the spiral notebooks and different kinds of pens. I finally chose a pink binder, paper with college-ruled lines, and dividers so I could make separate sections for taking notes in my classes. Alexa put a pocket dictionary in our basket, and I got a fresh blank pad like the kind my grandfather always kept handy. I could never have enough pads of paper to fill up with ideas and notes on things I planned to investigate. We spent a long time in the candle aisle because it smelled so good. Like vanilla, rose, and cinnamon. Then I picked up a lockable file box for storing clues.

We saved the makeup aisle for last, since this was the first year we were allowed to wear any. "Light colors only, and no lip liner, mascara, or eye liner," my mom had warned. "If I can tell you're wearing makeup you've got too much on."

Alexa and I compared many different pale-colored lipsticks and glosses. We opened one tester after another, twisting the product out of each tube and examining each color. She picked up a spicy red Cover Girl lipstick and showed it to me. "With your dark hair and fair skin you would look so glam in this."

"Like my mom would ever let me wear a dark color like that." Alexa shrugged and put it back. She ended up buying a light peach-colored lip gloss that was also peach scented and flavored, and I got shimmering cherry pink. We bought little makeup mirrors and breath mints, in case there were any cute boys in our classes. Most importantly, Dustin Coles for me, and Brendan Tadman for her. Every time I thought about Dustin my heart sped up. When Alexa saw him and he asked where I was, that meant something important: Dustin Coles cared what I was doing over the summer! I'd waited almost three months to see him again, and middle school was finally about to start.

Alexa was nervous too. She liked his BF Brendan, and so did all the popular girls in school who weren't crushing on Dustin. Brendan was really cute and a total crack-up. He'd make these crazy comments that were so hilarious you just about wet your pants laughing. Brendan had thick blondish-brown hair and amazing light brown eyes. They were kind of golden, like a tiger's. The only bad thing was, he didn't pay any attention to Alexa. He was the cutest boy in elementary school besides Dustin, and neither one of them were interested in us in sixth grade. This semester we were determined to change their minds.

That night I raced back and forth between my bedroom and my office, trying to get my backpack ready. I kept forgetting things I needed for my notebook pouch, and ran up and down the spiral stairs several times to grab a ruler or my new calculator. When I finally thought I had everything I needed, I realized I hadn't packed anything to write with.

When I thought about bedtime, sleep sounded impossible.

Could I find my way around Pacific and get to my classes on time? Would my teachers be cool—or not? Then a hideous thought hit me: *Would a certain blonde bully who had hated my guts since fifth grade be in any of my classes?* Thinking about her made my temples hurt. I called Alexa and she picked up instantly like she was hoping I'd get in touch.

"Hi Lex. It's almost here. Are you ready?"

"I have a stomachache."

"Probably just nerves. I'm nervous too."

"You don't have nearly as much to worry about," Alexa said softly. "You don't have a giant secret you're trying to keep from three-hundred other kids—or a thousand. Who could figure it out at any second, point, laugh, and make you the fool of the school."

"They won't," was all I could think of to say. Hoping I was right, and knowing I wasn't.

Alexa barked a fake laugh. "You know how to read."

"You do too," I tried to reassure her, as if she was being silly.

Alexa knew I was lying. She exhaled into the phone. "Barely."

When she started school in a tiny town in Texas, Alexa's first grade teacher told her parents she had Attention Deficit Disorder and wasn't paying attention, and that's why she was having trouble learning how to read and spell. Her teacher said she wasn't trying hard enough. Then she moved to California. Our second grade teacher noticed Alexa had trouble recognizing and writing letters, and suggested she get tested for a learning disability called *dyslexia*.

He was right: Alexa was dyslexic. She got some tutoring after school but she said it didn't help much, and her father never forgot what her first grade teacher said. "You have to try harder!" her dad would insist. Alexa told me more than once that if I hadn't been in her class, helping her study and explaining our assignments, she would have failed English.

"I'll help you," I said, realizing it wasn't enough.

"I know, but you can't take my tests or do my homework for me. And Ronnie told me I'd better be ready. Middle school is way harder than sixth grade." Alexa's big brother would rather be rock climbing or hiking up a mountain than doing homework, so maybe middle school had been hard for him. But he still shouldn't have scared her like that. "I have to get at least a *C* in English. My dad keeps telling me I need to apply myself more. He still doesn't understand that I'm trying as hard as I can." Her voice caught and she got quiet. "I just hope I can understand the textbooks. And I'm so afraid I'll make a fool of myself if we have to read out loud."

Stumbling over easy words made her feel stupid, and she was anything but dumb. Her brain just couldn't process what was written on the page. "We probably won't have to," I said. "Not in seventh grade, right?"

"Yeah, they probably figure we should be able to read by now," Alexa mumbled, and my heart sank.

I hadn't meant to hurt her feelings. "Want to share our lockers? Then we'll always see each other between classes," I said, hoping to cheer her up. "And you can help me find my way around Pacific." Maybe the thought of us helping each other would make her feel better.

"OK," Alexa agreed, knowing how easily I got lost. "That's a great idea. Tomorrow I'll meet you in first period, then we can find our lockers at the break."

"I better finish getting my stuff ready. See you in the morning. If I can find the building," I said, picking the corner of my pillow.

"You will. I'm more worried about what'll happen once we go inside." I heard Alexa take a deep breath.

I took one too. "See you tomorrow."

6
The First Day of Middle School

As soon as my alarm went off I bolted out of bed without hitting the snooze button once. My stomach flipped over. *The first day of middle school!* After my shower I put on the outfit I picked out the night before, grabbed my backpack, and ran downstairs to the kitchen. My mom's back was turned as she fussed with a stack of folders she planned to take to work.

"Ready," I announced.

"Not so fast, Kiddo," she said, setting down a bowl of oatmeal with sliced strawberries on top. My dad was sitting at the table, reading the paper and sipping coffee. He was working from home so he could keep an eye on the guys who were ripping out some of our old appliances and the rain gutters and putting in new ones. There was no way he would leave me home alone after school with a bunch of strangers. My mom wanted to keep the hundred-year-old countertops with yellowed tiles featuring a tiny flowered print. Fortunately the ancient wood paneling would be replaced by smooth drywall, ready for paint. The crumbling exterior also needed major help. I realized later that my dad keeping his eye on the construction crew was a great idea.

"Mom, I am so not hungry."

"You're just stressing because it's the first day at your new school." My mom handed me a spoon and a glass of orange juice. "It'll help if you eat something."

"All right," I grumbled. As soon as I took the first bite

I realized I was starving. "I just hope I'm not late."

My mom smiled. "Relax, Honey. We have plenty of time." The doorbell rang and my dad stood up and walked through the living room to answer the door. I heard loud voices and booted feet come through the entryway. Then banging and crunching noises as heavy tools were set down. The construction crew had arrived. While I was eating, my mom disappeared into a hallway and came back with something hideous hanging off the end of her stiff arm. "Here you go."

I looked up and my stomach bottomed out. "Oh *please* don't make me wear that." She gave me an annoyed look and shook the bulky sweater at me. Like she would ever wear something that ugly. "*Mom*, I'm starting a new school."

"Skylar."

I stared at her, horrified. "But I've had that sweater since fifth grade."

"It was big on you then, and it still fits," she said, sensibly.

"Mom, that thing's vile. And there's going to be boys at Pacific. Older ones." There would be hotties in my grade, too. Like Dustin.

Lines deepened in her forehead. "Middle school boys aren't going to protect you from the cold, Skylar." She draped the sweater over one of my shoulders.

Time to change up my strategy. "It's going to be eighty degrees today, Mom."

"And it's sixty-five now and breezy. Please hurry up and put it on. If you keep arguing with me you *are* going to be late."

Yanking thick, itchy wool around my shoulders I grumbled, "Could anything make me look like a bigger tool?" She didn't answer. Just walked toward the garage, looking over her shoulder to make sure I was coming.

Before I followed her I snuck a peek into the living room. It looked like Harley-Davidson was having a party. Beefy men with beards and tattoos lurked around, ready to start working but like they weren't sure what to do. A short, angry guy peered into every corner as if he was looking for something. I knew my parents would never have hired a scroungy crew like that if our next-door neighbor hadn't raved about the great job they had done on her house. She'd showed off her kitchen to my parents, who agreed that it looked amazing. Their prices were fair, too. However, I found out later that there were other details about the men that our new neighbor did not share with my mom and dad.

She beeped the horn. I headed for the garage, glancing over my shoulder at my dad who was watching the strange crew roam around our new house. We didn't talk much as we wound down the hill and drove past the beach, heading toward Pacific Middle School. After begging her to drop me off around the corner so no one would see me getting a ride from my mommy, I walked up to the entrance of the school I had been so looking forward to starting. My first day of seventh grade wasn't turning out to be nearly as fun as I had imagined.

Pacific was huge compared to elementary school. I had to find my way to six rooms in different buildings, and I didn't know where any of them were. Worse yet, a breeze came up and it *was* cold, so I kept the sweater on.

If someone started a Worst Dressed list, I'd be number one. My face was hot, my stomach felt jumpy, and my hands were sweating. How pathetic.

Looking around, I didn't see Alexa or one single person I knew. I wanted to get to my first class before the other girls noticed me wandering around alone, wondered why I didn't have any friends, and decided there must be something wrong with me. I wouldn't have admitted it to anybody, but I was scared to death. Then a worse thought hit me: If I wasn't even brave enough to make it through the first day of middle school, how could I run my own detective agency?

One of my undercover detective fantasies took over and I tried to get my confidence back.

I walked through a glamorous hotel wearing high heels, a short blonde wig, and brown contact lenses. A sparkling chandelier dangled from the ceiling and knots of foreign businessmen bustled around me. I was wired with an earpiece, a microphone, and a recording device, ready to eavesdrop on a secret meeting of anti-American forces. Suddenly enemy agents in suits and dark sunglasses rushed through the lobby, heading straight for me. Before they could catch me I darted into an elevator, came back out disguised as a man, and escaped into a waiting limousine.

"Private detectives aren't chicken," I mumbled to myself.

Yeah, right.

I finally found room A-12 just as Alexa rushed around the corner. "Hurry," I said, and she caught up to me right as the warning bell rang.

"I went to room A-21 by mistake. I thought it said

43

A-12," she admitted, and her cheeks turned pink.

"It's OK. Come on."

We walked inside the classroom and I couldn't believe what I saw. I grabbed Alexa's arm and pointed toward the fourth row with my eyes. *Dustin Coles was in our first class.* She steered me down the first aisle and I could almost feel Alexa vibing me not to look at him. But, *OMG,* he got so tan over the summer. And Dustin had actually asked Alexa where I was, *twice.* Once at the party I'd missed and once when she ran into him at the mall. *Did the biggest hottie in Santa Monica really care what I was doing before we came back to school?*

Apparently not. Dustin barely looked up when I walked in. He glanced at me and nodded his head in the fastest *hello* possible. Then the boy on his other side started talking to him and he turned away, just as I started walking down the aisle toward the fourth row. Maybe when Dustin asked Alexa about me during the break he was just trying to think of something to say. My heart sank as I realized he probably wasn't interested in me after all.

There weren't any empty desks near him anyway. I looked around the room, hoping I wouldn't spot my enemy. And then my stomach lurched. *There she was.* On Dustin's other side. The bully who had hated my guts for two years: Emelyn Peters.

I remembered the first day that Emelyn came to our elementary school from Florida, sneering as she looked around, complaining about the shabby classroom.

"They wouldn't put up with these conditions in West Palm Beach," Emelyn said, sticking her pointy nose into the

air and flipping white-blonde hair over one shoulder.

"What's wrong with it?" I asked innocently.

"Yeah, what's wrong with it?" Alexa put her hands on her hips.

Emelyn whirled around and glared at us, and her eyes narrowed. "This school is a total dump. *But it figures* you two *wouldn't get it."*

That was our first taste of Emelyn Peters. She'd grown up rich and spoiled, until her dad got sent to prison for stealing money from the company where he worked. Then Emelyn moved to California with her mom and her tall, blond older brother and started acting like the queen of our elementary school. When her brother got suspended from Pacific for selling marijuana, Emelyn bragged about it to everybody like he was really cool. Then she started crushing on Dustin and things got ugly.

In fifth grade Alexa, Emelyn, Dustin, and I had all been in the same class. Alexa's best subject was art, and one day we all had to sketch each other in charcoal. My picture of Alexa came out okay, but her drawing looked *exactly* like me. The teacher hung it on the bulletin board with the other best ones. Dustin looked at Alexa's sketch and then at me. "You look better up there than in real life." Dustin was trying to tease me, but when he realized it sounded like a compliment, he blushed. Emelyn Peters glared at me like she wanted to rip my hair out—then, and any time Dustin had talked to me since. She got suspended twice last year for bullying, but it didn't do any good. Emelyn was as mean as ever. She wasn't afraid of anything or anyone, and she let us all know it.

Alexa and I couldn't find two chairs next to each other, so she had to sit one row over and two seats back. I looked over my shoulder and Emelyn pointed at me and blew her cheeks out like a bloated fish, which was exactly what I felt like in my fifth-grade sweater. *Thanks, Mom.* Why hadn't I stuffed the stupid thing in my locker when I had the chance? Ripping it from around my shoulders, I tried to cram it into my backpack but it didn't fit. I hung the sweater on the back of my chair and could almost feel everyone behind me staring at its ugliness.

The teacher hobbled in and wrote her name on the board. "Good morning, class, I'm Mrs. Mintin." Mrs. Mintin wore her gray hair in a tight bun, and she walked slowly as if her pointy shoes hurt her feet. "Everyone please take out a sheet of paper. I'd like you all to write two paragraphs describing a problem you had over the summer, and how you solved it. You have twenty minutes. Begin."

After thinking for a minute, I wrote a long paragraph about how we had to move out of our old house and into a new one. My problem was that I fell in love with this old stone mansion we'd seen, but my mom thought it was too old and dirty and not worth the money. I described how I'd solved the problem by using good arguments to convince my mom to buy the house. Like the greenhouse could be her hideaway, I wouldn't have to change school districts, and we'd still be close to both my parents' jobs. My essay practically wrote itself and I was done in less than ten minutes.

With time to kill, I took out my notepad and glanced at everyone sitting near me, but there wasn't anybody exciting enough to write comments about. I debated playing Silent Detective solitaire, where I check out an interesting person and write down what I think their favorite food is, what they want to be when they grow up, and what they like to do when they're all by themselves. Then I try to get to know them and find out if I'm right. But I already knew the boy next to me, and the girls on my right were pretty average and didn't spark my curiosity.

I decided to do a little spying and fished my compact out of my purse. Opening up the mirror, I angled it so I could see the fourth row of desks over my shoulder. Dustin was close to the end of that row, but his head was bent over his paper so I couldn't see his face. Better not to stare at him anyway. He'd probably look up and catch me. Angling my mirror in the other direction, I pretended to look at myself while I put on lip gloss, but I was really checking on Alexa. Her knees bounced up and down as she frowned at her paper with an angry look on her face. I knew she was willing the words to come, but her pencil wasn't moving.

I also knew the people sitting near her couldn't help her with her spelling like I would have. They didn't know the secret code we'd made up in fourth grade: Alexa would tap her pencil on her desk twice, then whisper a word to herself, just loud enough for me to hear. I glance around the classroom casually to make sure the teacher isn't looking at us. Then I would bend over my paper and whisper the spelling to Alexa. We never considered it cheating since Alexa was competing with such a disadvantage. I was just helping her catch up to the rest of the class. But a new teacher probably wouldn't see it that way.

I'd helped Alexa try to hide her dyslexia from our classmates since we were nine, but the older we got the harder it was to fake everyone out. Since last year I've tried to figure out how to help her deal with it instead.

All of a sudden Alexa doubled over in pain. I put down the mirror and turned around to look at her. She raised her hand and asked to be excused, and then hurried out of the room. *Did she have another stomachache? Or was she trying to get out of writing the essay?* Maybe she was afraid we'd have to read our paragraphs out loud and she'd feel embarrassed. I wanted to chase after her to see if she was all right, but I didn't want to make the teacher mad.

Peeking back into my mirror, I saw Emelyn Peters point at the door and snicker with a tough girl named Pat Whitehead who sat on her other side. Pat's hair was short on the sides and spiked up in the middle with gel. Her eyes were so light-colored they looked like an albino rat's. Pat had four brothers, and the five Whiteheads were always getting into fights. "Dyslexa had to *GO*," Pat said, and Emelyn bent over her desk laughing loudly. Spying on those two was anything but fun. I put my mirror back inside my purse, wishing I were home looking for clues to find the hidden jewels.

If I had any idea what was already starting to happen at my house I would have been glad to be safe and sound, writing a paragraph in English class.

At lunch I met Alexa at our locker. She smiled, but her face didn't look happy. "Are you OK?" I asked.

"Yeah. My stomach was killing me so I went to the bathroom and then to the nurse's office. She called my mom and then gave me a Tylenol."

"Did it help?"

"Not really. I'm all right. Just hungry." We headed for the cafeteria and Alexa nudged me. "Look," she whispered. Dustin and Brendan were just a few tables away. Dustin's green shirt really made his eyes stand out, and Brendan was leaning over the table, waving his arms like he was telling a funny story. Emelyn and her friends were sitting right behind them, giggling loudly and trying to get their attention.

I looked at Alexa and rolled my eyes. "Emelyn makes me lose my appetite."

She nodded. "Her whole table is trouble."

After school I took the bus most of the way home. Sitting on the grass by the sidewalk, I checked Facebook and email on my phone while I waited for my mom to pick me up at the bottom of the hill. The waves were flat, so there were no explosive crashes when they broke. Just a quiet sizzle followed by a long *shhhhh* as the water moved slowly forward and back across the sand. Then I tried to study history, jiggling my foot, reading the same paragraph over and over. The first day of school had me so wired I could barely concentrate.

Dustin Coles was in two of my classes! Fortunately Emelyn Peters was only in one. *And there were clues to a fortune hidden somewhere in my new house.* I hoped an aggressive bunch of construction workers wouldn't get in the way of my search. I was also hoping my mom would get there soon so I could get back to work on the mystery, but as soon as she pulled over I wished she'd forgotten to come get me. "Hi Skylar," my mom said as I swung my legs into the car. "Where's your sweater?"

"Uh," I stalled, trying to remember where I'd seen it last. "I'm not sure."

She threw the gearshift into park and turned to face me. "Don't tell me you lost it." I could tell by the way her eyebrows were pinched together that she thought I *lost* it on purpose.

"Wait. Let me think. It's not in my locker, and it didn't fit in my backpack." I could reason this out if she'd just give me a minute. "I had it in first period but I don't remember having it at the break. I must have left it in English." It was probably still hanging on the back of the chair. No way would anyone steal something that ugly.

"That's convenient. You didn't want to wear it this morning and now it's missing." My mom put the car in gear and steered carefully into traffic.

"I didn't lose it on purpose." She glanced at me with one eyebrow raised. "I *didn't*. I'm sure I'll find it tomorrow. If it isn't in English I'll try the Lost and Found."

"Let's hope you do find it, or its replacement is coming out of your chores money."

Delightful.

A few minutes later we pulled into our driveway. We sat silently while the garage door opened. "I needed a new one anyway," I mumbled.

"No you didn't."

7
My Detective Kit

After my mom reminded me to check the Lost and Found first thing in the morning I raced up the two sets of stairs to my bedroom. Downstairs, our house was full of workmen. All six of them looked dirty and sweaty. Most of them had ugly colorless tattoos on their arms: snakes and crosses and skulls with empty eye sockets. Some of the guys were installing new light fixtures and others were putting in curtains and blinds. They had taken down all the old ones and had carried many loads of junk to the dumpster we'd rented. The whole bottom floor smelled like B.O. The men were all working hard. Except one.

I knew who the foreman was, because he bossed everyone around but didn't seem to do any work himself. It was the short, angry-looking guy I'd spotted before school. His name was Barney, but the workers all called him Smack. I guess if my name were Barney I'd use a nickname too. Smack was no taller than me, but he was very wide and had giant shoulders and one squinty eye. The way he walked with his legs far apart reminded me of a pirate. He had a squeaky voice, and there was something fishy about the way he moved around our house. Every now and then he would look over his shoulder or snoop around in our stuff for a minute. I planned to keep my eye on Smack.

Once I was back inside my room I dumped my backpack on my bed, closed the door, and burned vanilla incense. I wanted to hurry and finish unpacking so I could start my search for Xandra Collins's clues. On our first night in the new house I had taken a quick look through all the rooms on every floor, and didn't find a thing except rat turds and bird droppings. But it didn't surprise me; I didn't expect clues to be neatly folded on shelves in the library or resting inside a bowl in the kitchen. I knew this was going to take some work. And according to the mysterious note, it would also take guts.

I worked at putting away my book collection first. My mom's old Nancy Drew and Trixie Belden mysteries were in the top of the first box. Sarah Dessen, Deb Caletti, and Meg Cabot novels made up the next layer, and I had tucked *Gilda Joyce: Psychic Investigator, Model Spy,* and some other hard covers around the sides. I ripped open the second box and unpacked my *Gallagher Girls* and *Amanda Project* paperbacks.

When I finished the third box and all my books were on their shelves, I looked around the small space and tried to decide how to arrange my new bedroom. My summer friend Kat had a cool room in a beachfront house in Shadow Hills. Her bedroom was divided into four quadrants, one representing each element: earth, water, air, and fire. I decided to decorate mine the same way. "Grandpa's desk symbolizes earth, since it is made of wood. So the earth section will be the turret room." His antique desk was already up there, topped with orange, green, and brown candles and my fern. Perfect.

I moved a little marble table next to the wall and put my desktop fountain on top of it. "This is the water quadrant." Running into the closest bathroom to fill a glass, I poured water into the fountain and turned it on, smiling when the water began to trickle over the rocks. I hammered a little nail into the wall behind the fountain and hung up the Dream Catcher I made in summer school. I had woven little shells in between knots of blue-green yarn around a circular frame. Maybe I'd get a couple of black goldfish and put seashells from the beach around the bottom of their bowl.

"The air section can be over here." I set my glass butterfly figurine on a shelf by the window and planned to make a mobile out of feathers, twigs, and string that would spin in the breeze. "Now for fire." I arranged candles on the top of my little bookcase, and finished the fire quad with my new incense burner.

Then I took out my favorite possession besides Grandpa's badge: my detective kit. There were places in our new house that I could investigate using each item. The jumbo flashlight would be perfect for exploring the backyard, the hillside, and the hidden floor, after I found it. My pocket penlight would light up the shadowy corners of the bedrooms and my office, the insides of cupboards, and other secret spots where clues might be hidden. Black light flashlight: useful everywhere. I could see blood, fingerprints, and invisible ink when I shined its ultraviolet light in the dark.

My laser pointer shot a red beam of light across the room. It was really only useful for pointing at things or for blinding myself or someone else, according to my mom. If she knew how I had actually used it to defend myself over the summer it would have curled her toes.

There were protective gloves and goggles, and a

measuring tape, pen, and sketchpad for taking notes at crime scenes. I had a magnifying glass that I used to look for clues, tweezers to pick them up with, and evidence envelopes to put them in. When I got home from Shadow Hills, the listening device I'd sent away for had finally come. My Soundtrap was a directional microphone that was the size and shape of a new pencil, connected to a pair of earbuds. Perfect for eavesdropping. I'd saved up my chores and weeding money for months to pay for it and it was worth every quarter.

My favorite detective tool was my fingerprinting kit. It had black and white dusting powder for finding fingerprints, a brush to dust on the powder, and clear strips of tape for lifting the prints. There were Case Solution cards to paste fingerprints or other clues onto, which I labeled with invisible ink. And of course I had my pink, Super-Zoom binoculars. I would probably need every single item in my kit to help me find Xandra's hidden jewels.

My Porta-detective kit contained a miniature set of spy tools. It was a pink metal carryall with leopard spots that looked like a lunch box, so I could take it to school and stay undercover. You never knew when your detective gear would come in handy.

When I got sick of unpacking I took a break and decided to make a sign for my office door. First I carried my art supplies and detective kit up the stairs and sat down at my desk. Grabbing a ruler, I drew pencil lines on a piece of white poster board. Then I used my stencil to draw the letters, and colored them in using marking pens in different shades of violet and blue. I decorated the borders with pink and purple glitter ink.

"Perfect," I said, holding up my sign and admiring my work. I hung it on the turret room door with heavy-duty pushpins.

The Skylar Robbins Detective Agency

Open for business! I opened the note-taking app and typed, "The Mystery of the Hidden Jewels." If I could solve this mystery, maybe my agency would finally get famous. I liked to fantasize about going on exciting missions, deep undercover.

I was seated at a formal table in a castle dining room next to the highest member of a Middle Eastern government. A microphone the size of a pinhead hid under a button on my silk blouse, and a micro-camera disguised as a jewel dangled from my necklace. I flirted with my handsome enemy until he was distracted, then dropped a pill into his drink. When the drug loosened his lips he revealed a plan to attack the United States, which I recorded. I brought the Top Secret information back to America, revealed the plot to the FBI, and prevented a terrorist attack.

The fantasy evaporated when a horrible banging sound made me jump right out of my chair. I hurried over to the window and looked down into the yard, spotting a construction worker with a black beard and muscles so big he looked like a professional wrestler. He was ripping broken wood trim and the old rain gutter off of our house. I'd heard Smack's squeaky voice yelling at him earlier. His name was Sledge. Picking up a huge pile of junk, Sledge groaned loudly as he heaved it into the dumpster. Then he snooped around the backyard for a minute, glancing over his shoulder to see if anyone was watching him.

Sledge cracked his knuckles and peeked into the gazebo. When he looked up at the turret, I dropped to my knees so I wouldn't get caught spying. The cleaning crew had obviously missed the turret room, because the windowsill was covered with dust. I had just started to stand up when something caught my eye.

There was a pattern in the dust.

I looked at it more closely and my heart started to pound. I stood up, snatching my detective kit off the floor. Plucked out my magnifying glass and studied the windowsill through it. I sucked in my breath and the hair stood up on my arms.

I had just found the first clue.

8
Invisible Ink

ingerprints covered the entire length of the dirty sill. *Whose are they?* I wondered. *Xandra Collins's? Or maybe her kidnapper's?*

Somebody left a trace.

My round office had tall, narrow windows all the way around it, stopping only for the doorway, a cupboard, and a couple of feet on each side of the door. A curving windowsill ran all the way around the wall. Grabbing the flashlight out of my detective kit, I shined the light on the windowsill and looked at it through my magnifying glass. The prints were pressed down one after the other in a rambling line that led to the end of the sill. Then the fingerprints stopped.

My eyes darted around the room, looking for more clues. I didn't find any. Then I looked at the sill through my mag glass, picking up the trail. The prints climbed the wall and stopped right below the cupboard. These were no random fingerprints in dust. These were made on purpose. *How could Xandra's heirs have missed this?*

My conscience poked me. *You missed it too—until now.*

I opened the cupboard door.

It was empty.

Shining my big flashlight inside, I stuck my entire head into the cupboard, but all I could see was spider webs, dust, and a dead fly. Was the dead fly a clue? I didn't think so. But the fingerprints had stopped.

Was that it? Weren't the prints a clue after all? I was sure someone had pressed them into the dirt so they led to the cupboard for a reason. But why?

I needed to get out my black light and shine it in there to see if I could find something that wasn't visible otherwise. Like maybe there would be faded blood beneath the dirt. I shined the ultraviolet light inside, and then I stopped moving and stared.

A message was written on the wall in invisible ink.

Congratulations. You found the first clue.

Here is your second clue: Things in this room are not always what they seem.

I whirled around with my heart hammering, almost expecting to see Xandra's ghost or nosy Smack standing behind me.

No one was there.

9
A Tattered, Yellowed Envelope

Taking a deep breath, I forced myself to calm down and think. A detective rule my grandfather taught me popped into my mind: *Always remember that crime scenes are three-dimensional. Look for clues on the floor, all four walls, and the ceiling.* I searched my office, looking for something that might not be as it seemed.

My office was tiny. I finished in just a few minutes and didn't find a thing. A second bang echoed from the backyard. I flinched and stood still, waiting for another sound. Nothing happened. It was too quiet.

Dropping to my knees, I crawled back over to the window and peeked out over the sill. Sledge was slinking around the yard with a piece of rain gutter in his hand, peering into every corner while he pretended to be working. He was spending a lot more time looking around than installing rain gutters. *Hmm.*

No time to waste watching him.

I went back to the cupboard and read the second clue again.

Things in this room are not always what they seem.

Pushing my desk chair over to the wall and standing on it, I shined the flashlight back into the cupboard. Then I stuck my whole upper body inside, twisting around and looking at the back of the front wall, and feeling all over. The cupboard was definitely empty. But when I reached up and pushed on the cupboard's ceiling, it flexed. I aimed my flashlight up there and saw a thin seam around the edges. Shining the light into the corners, I noticed four screws that had been painted to match the dull beige of the cupboard.

The cupboard had a false ceiling.

I ran down two flights of stairs, hoping to find a friendly workman.

A thin guy named Ignado who had greasy black hair was threading heavy curtains onto a rod in the living room. I looked at his leather tool belt while he and a pale man with bags under his eyes balanced the rod and lifted it onto big brackets. Ignado finally noticed that I was watching him and turned to look at me. One of his eyes was brown and the other was a cloudy blue. The blue-gray right eye didn't follow his left one. It reminded me of Alexa's old dog when it went blind.

I cleared my throat. "Excuse me, but can I borrow your screwdriver for a second?" Ignado looked at me suspiciously like he wondered why I wanted to use his tool. "I'm trying to hang a picture, and I need to screw in a hook," I fibbed. "I'll bring it right back."

"No problem," he said, handing it to me slowly. "I ain't using it." When I smiled at Ignado I got a smirk in return.

"Thank you," I said, backing away from him.

I ran up the two flights of stairs and up my spiral staircase. By the time I got to the top of the turret I was out of breath. Standing on my chair, I aimed the flashlight at one corner of the ceiling and started to work on the screws. The paint made them really hard to turn, but I finally got all four of them out. Then I pushed the top of the cupboard up, turned it on its side, and lowered it through the opening.

My heart started to pound. Above where the false ceiling had been, a tattered, yellowed envelope was taped to the wall.

Just as I reached for the envelope, "Skylar? *Skylar!*" my father shouted from somewhere below me. "We need your help downstairs. Now please." I could tell by the sound of his voice that he meant *right* now. It sounded like he was standing in the hall outside my bedroom, so I scrambled off my chair and closed the cupboard door, leaving the mysterious envelope taped high up inside.

I hurried down the stairs so I could return the screwdriver before helping my dad. Ignado gave me a creepy smile. "How'd it go?" he asked, focusing on me with his brown eye while the cloudy blue one stared blindly into the area above my head.

"Good. Thanks," I said, handing him the screwdriver while I took a quick look around the raw, dusty room.

He held onto the tool, staring at me hard before he pulled the screwdriver away from me. "Be careful," he said, wrapping a dirty hank of hair behind his ear.

"Of what?" I asked, wondering if this was some kind of a threat.

"Remodels can be real dangerous," he warned as a bald guy with a huge belly let a thick beam crash loudly to the floor.

I had to load kitchen cupboards right up to dinnertime. Then we unpacked books in the library until it was time to go to bed. I kissed my parents goodnight, changed into my nightgown, and brushed my teeth. After turning out my light, I opened my detective kit and groped around in the dark until I found my penlight. Then I crept up the spiral staircase and tiptoed across my office floor.

Quietly opening the cupboard door, I stood on my chair and aimed my penlight beam at the false ceiling. Stretching my arm up as high as I could reach, I moved the panel to the side and snatched the yellowed envelope down off the wall.

It looked old and was stained, and some of the corners had been nibbled away by rats, roaches, or something even more disgusting. I pried open the flap, hoping to find a treasure map that would lead me to Xandra's jewelry box. I pulled out an old piece of unlined paper, and carefully unfolded it.

"What could this possibly mean?" I asked the shadows.

10
Not Exactly a Kiss

The next morning I took one last look at the puzzling clue, then rushed downstairs and ate breakfast. No time to figure it out now. I had another mystery to solve.

My mom drove me to school, and I hurried to room A-12 and walked up to my English teacher's desk before the bell rang. Mrs. Mintin was reading the school newspaper. "Excuse me," I said, waiting for her to look up. "Um, I left my sweater on the back of my chair yesterday. Did anyone turn it in?" I tried not to wiggle impatiently like I had to go to the bathroom.

She stared at me over the top of her reading glasses. "No, but a friend of yours took it with her after class. She probably looked after it for you and will return it today." Mrs. Mintin looked back at her paper like the discussion had ended.

Fine with me. Now I could get my mom off my back. "Alexa took it?"

"I'm not sure. I haven't memorized all of the students' names yet. Please take your seat." Maybe Alexa had taken it and just forgot to tell me. I sat down, feeling better about everything.

For a second-and-a-half.

"Hey, Skylar." Brendan Tadman slid into the chair next to mine.

OK, I thought, *this is cool. But why is Brendan Tadman talking to me?*

He leaned across the aisle with a curious expression on his face. Like he was trying not to laugh. "Interesting place to hang your sweater. At least I think it's yours."

Oh-oh.

"What are you talking about?" I looked at him with a queasy feeling rolling around in my stomach.

"Beige? Kind of big and thick?"

I saw embarrassment in my immediate future. "That sounds like mine. Uh—where is it?" I felt my cheeks turning pink, then red.

Brendan looked toward the window and laughed. "Put it this way: sweaters seem to be growing on trees near the cafeteria."

Terrific.

I didn't have time to check between classes, so at the ten o'clock break I hurried toward the lunch area. There was a big patch of lawn in front of the outdoor tables with three palm trees and some tall pines and oaks growing around the sides. I looked up. Sure enough, someone had flung my ugly sweater way up into one of the oak trees. I had to find out who had chucked it up there. Probably a certain blonde from Florida.

I hurried back to Mrs. Mintin's room, poked my head inside the door, and looked around. She was sitting at her desk grading papers. It took me a minute to get my guts up and walk inside. I had to stand in front of her desk for like seven seconds before she looked at me. "Yes?"

"Mrs. Mintin, whoever took my sweater yesterday threw it up into one of the trees by the cafeteria."

She squinted at me over the rim of her glasses and patted her hair, which was stiff with spray. "Well, why

64

don't you wait until lunch and ask the janitor to help you get it down? I'm sure he has a long pole or a ladder."

"OK. But I need to know who left with it yesterday. Alexa is the girl in the second-to-last row with long, curly strawberry blonde hair and freckles. It wasn't her, was it?"

Mrs. Mintin shook her head. "No. It was the pretty blonde who sits in the back row." She opened a desk drawer and glanced at a seating chart. "Emelyn Peters took your sweater. I thought she intended to return it."

I felt my fingernails dig into my palms. "No, that isn't what she intended at all."

Lunch was going to be fun.

After fourth period Alexa and I headed straight for the cafeteria and talked while we walked. "So there's this gross bunch of guys remodeling our house."

Alexa looked at me. "Gross how?" She pushed open the door and I followed her over to the tray table. The air was thick with steam and French fry grease.

"Sweaty bikers. They stink. And that's the least of it."

"Stink as bad as those green beans?" Alexa asked, making a face as we passed a metal warming bin heaped full of limp vegetables. The guy behind us slid his tray forward and made a disgusted grunt.

"Worse," I said. We walked over to the lasagna counter and a stocky lady wearing a stained red apron served each of us a gooey rectangular slice. I took a breath, thinking about the construction workers. "They're rude. And they make me nervous. Like I'm working for them, instead of the other way around. They act like it's their house, not mine. And there's something fishy about them. The foreman, Smack? He seems like he's always snooping—"

"Smack?" Alexa laughed, reaching for a salad.

"His real name's Barney."

"Aha. Nickname. So why don't you just ignore them?"

"Wish I could, but they're all up in our stuff for one. And they seem like they're up to something besides remodeling our house."

Alexa looked at me. She bit a nail. "Like what?"

"I'm not sure. But something about them seems bent."

"Not good," she said, stepping up to the cashier and opening her purse.

"No. It's not," I agreed, reaching into my wallet.

"Why did your parents hire them, then?" she asked, wrinkling her nose.

"They made a low bid, and they came highly recommended by our neighbor. Who my mom had known for about five seconds."

"Huh. Kind of fishy."

"Yeah."

"You'll figure it out," Alexa said, paying the cashier and leading the way outside.

I wished I were as confident.

We sat down at an empty table and I took a bite of lasagna. Molten cheese burned my mouth and I gulped water, trying to cool it off. A few minutes later I was playing with a dangling strip of fried skin with my tongue.

I'd hoped to get my sweater out of the tree without attracting too much attention, but by the time we tracked down the skinny janitor the lunch area was packed. I spotted him emptying a garbage can in the corner. His straggly blond ponytail was turning gray, and his blue jumpsuit had *Frank* embroidered on the pocket in white stitches. Frank put a new liner into the can.

"Excuse me," I said, "but can you please help me get my sweater down? It's caught in a tree." The janitor seemed to think this was funny. "My English teacher said you might be able to help me. Like do you have a pole or a ladder or anything?"

"Sure, kid. What tree?" Frank had a giant, bobbing Adam's Apple. The corners of his mouth curled up and he shoved his hands into his pockets. We walked past the outdoor tables and I pointed out the oak.

"That one right there." My sweater hung off the end of a branch like a piece of rotten fruit. I heard girls giggling and opened up my Porta-detective kit. Pulling out a little round mirror, I cupped it in my palm, aiming it over my shoulder. I turned slowly sideways, scanning the lunch area behind me. Pat Whitehead and a snotty blonde named Trish Adams were eating at a table nearby.

"Hey look. Skylar's got a *hot date!*" Pat shouted. I wasn't about to let her intimidate me. Turning around, I looked at her and rolled my eyes. Trish made devil horns at me and opened her mouth, showing me a chewed bite of food. Emelyn was sitting at Dustin's table and she laughed at me as hard as she could. I waved nicely at her. Then I turned my back and ignored them.

But the janitor didn't. "Hey!" Frank barked, attracting all sorts of attention. "Simmer down!" he yelled. Now the entire lunch area watched us walk up to the tree. My cheeks were burning. Then Frank made everything worse. He actually shimmied right up the trunk like a monkey.

Brendan Tadman cupped his hands around his mouth and shouted, "Hey, are there any bananas up there?" Pat pointed at me and nudged Trish, and then they both cracked up. My cheeks were burning and I knew my face was as red as a tomato. Dustin actually looked like he felt sorry for me, so Emelyn tugged on his arm to make him pay attention to her instead. The janitor plucked my sweater off the branch and tossed it down to me. I caught it, and some of the kids who were watching hooted and clapped.

Lucky me. I had my sweater back.

After that Alexa and I walked to the bathroom. "How embarrassing was that?" I asked angrily, yanking a brush through my hair. "All because my mom made me wear that stupid sweater."

"Don't worry, everyone's already forgotten about it."

"Sure they have," I said. I knew Alexa was just trying to make me feel better by the way she fumbled around in her purse, fishing out her lip gloss instead of looking me in the eye. "I wish." I checked to make sure I didn't have lasagna stuck in my teeth, then put on some sheer pink Lipslick.

Walking into Science a few minutes early, I sat down at a lab table in the back of the room where the other chairs were empty. The class began to fill, and I didn't see any of my friends. Then I couldn't believe my luck. Dustin Coles walked in, his big green-brown eyes glancing around the room until he chose an empty seat—the one right next to mine! His wavy brown hair curled over his collar in back, and there were new blond streaks where the sun had highlighted it. Double yum.

OMG. His head turned toward me in slow motion, like in a PG-13, right before the boy kisses—

"Hi Skylar." He smiled at me. Not exactly a kiss, but definitely better than nothing. And when he said my name, it sounded really good.

"Hi." I hoped my face wasn't turning red. Dustin tapped his pen against the table and looked around the room. I tried to think of something interesting to say so I could keep talking to him but my brain farted out on me.

A second later the teacher walked in. Mr. Bidden was tall and stooped, and he had thin gray hair and a hooked nose. His skin was pale and wrinkled and covered with moles. The collar of his shirt was too big for his skinny neck, and he wore a white lab coat over his clothes. With the gray-green chalkboard behind him, he looked like a poster for some creepy hospital that would give you a worse disease than you came in with.

He set down a thick file and scowled at us. "We will study anatomy for the first two weeks of this semester. Please open your books to chapter one. Then read the directions for the first lab and choose partners. You need to form four-person teams and appoint a leader."

I read the first lines of the instructions: *Pick partners you are comfortable with. Students who object to the graphic nature of this experiment may opt out and complete a virtual version of the anatomy lab online.* I tried to swallow, but suddenly I couldn't work up any saliva. Graphic? *What were we going to have to do?* Scenes from a horror movie I'd watched recently flashed through my mind.

I glanced around, hoping to see something familiar or

pretty. A plant or a fish tank—something alive or calming. The metal tools on the sterile white counters were doing nothing for my nerves. Dustin read the directions and then looked across the room, trying to spot some of his friends. I guess none of his buds were in our class. He turned to face me. "Want to be one of my partners?"

No *way*. If anyone had told me Dustin Coles would ask me to be his lab partner I never would have believed it. I figured he'd try to pick the other popular guys to team up with, but he wasn't looking around anymore. I nodded, hoping my face wouldn't turn beet red and give me away. "OK. Do you want to be the team leader?"

"Sure," he agreed. "No problem." A skinny guy in a plaid shirt sat across from me. The blonde girl next to him wore glasses and looked too young to be in our grade. "How 'bout you guys," Dustin asked. "Want to team up?"

The girl nodded gratefully and the thin kid smiled and said, "Yeah." I could tell Dustin already had two new fans.

"I'm Dustin Coles," he said, confidently. "What're your guys' names?"

The girl looked at Dustin and her cheeks turned pink. "Cindy Kowalski."

"Mark Oglethorpe." He straightened in his chair.

"Skylar Robbins," I said, feeling silly that we were introducing ourselves so formally. My mom would have loved it.

"Welcome to the A Team," Dustin said, knocking knuckles with Mark, who was grinning his butt off to have the coolest guy in school choose him for a partner. Suddenly I didn't feel silly anymore. We spent the rest of the hour scribbling anatomy notes while Mr. Bidden lectured, and left the class with permission slips for our parents to sign by Friday.

11
The Third Clue

When I got into my mom's car after school she saw my sweater and smiled. "You found it."

"Yeah I found it. The whole school watched me find it."

"What?" She looked over her shoulder to check the traffic, and then glanced at me. "Where was it?"

"Up a tree."

"A tree? How did it get—"

"Don't ask. The janitor got it down for me." I turned to look at her. "Everyone clapped."

I didn't get any sympathy. "Well at least you don't have to buy a new one. And I'm sure you'll be more careful with your things from now on."

I wanted to tell her that Emelyn Peters had stolen it off the back of my chair before she flung it into the tree, but I was sick of arguing with my mom and bored with the subject of my pukey sweater. I decided to let her win this one. "OK, Mom."

After escaping from the garage, I ran up the stairs to my room and climbed the spiral staircase to my office. Homework could wait until later. I'd been looking forward to working on the third clue all day. Pushing my chair back over to the desk, I sat down and turned the yellowed envelope over in my hands. I pulled out the paper and unfolded it.

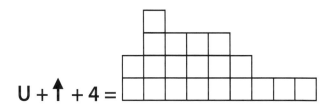

The drawing looked like a cross between an algebra problem and an optical illusion or a puzzle. I flipped through my math book and looked at the symbols in the geometry chapters. None of them matched the design on the clue. After staring at the tattered paper for a few minutes, I turned on my iPad and opened my Hidden Jewelry Box notes. After I took a picture of the clue I counted the squares, and then typed in: *Bottom row, 9. Next row, 6. Second row 4. Top row, 1.*

The diagram looked a little like a weird stairway or something you could climb, so the next thing I did was enter the directions the squares seemed to take to get from the bottom to the top of the puzzle: *4 to the left, up 1. 1 more to the left, up 1. 3 to the left, up to the top.* Now I was at the top of…what? I blew out my breath. I was usually good at puzzles and math, but this didn't make any sense at all.

What could it mean? I posted a picture of the clue on my website, then sent out a tweet asking for my agents to check in and help. I hoped agent # 010 Star Dancer or # 002 Hidden Shadow might be online to post their ideas on my site under *clues.*

Next, I typed just the numbers of the squares in each row: 9 6 4 1

"Nine minus six is three, and four minus one is three."

Then I added the numbers up. "Twenty squares," I said, looking at the equation on the clue. "*U* plus arrow plus four equals twenty. Sixteen plus four equals twenty, so *U* plus arrow equals sixteen. But what does that mean?" I groaned in frustration. "Nothing," I answered myself.

I grabbed my head with both hands. *Now what do I do?* I had no idea what the third clue meant, or where to look for the next one. I stared at the frayed paper.

That's when I saw it. A curly black hair, resting innocently on my desk. Except there was nothing innocent about it. My dad's hair was light. My mom and I didn't have hairy arms or legs. Therefore this came from someone else. Someone with dark curly hair, like Sledge: the guy in the construction crew gang who was working on our rain gutters.

Crew Gang, I thought. Good name for that bunch of creeps.

I stared at the little hair and my face got hot. What was he doing in my office? No rain gutters up here, no reason for him to be in this room at all. Unless he was snooping. Searching for something, like when I'd watched him peek into the gazebo and look into the corners of our backyard. I clamped my hand over my mouth as the truth dawned on me.

Those guys are looking for the hidden jewels too.

Xandra Collins's missing jewelry box had been all over the news since her disappearance. It made perfect sense that the men working on our house would be searching for her jewelry box. And there was a whole gang of them. Only one of me.

I had to beat them to it. I was one step ahead of them,

and I needed to stay that way. Picking up the hair with my tweezers, I dropped it into a small Ziploc baggie and stowed it in my detective kit. DNA evidence, in case I needed it.

The clue sat there, challenging me.

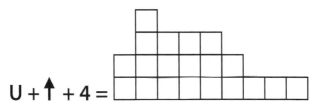

What did the squares stand for? Could they represent a building? And if they did, how would I find it? I didn't have a truck like Smack. No way I could search all of Santa Monica on my bike. Fortunately Alexa and a gang of secret agents were on my side. The Shirley Lock Holmes Agency could track a clue faster than anybody. Girls Secret Agency had gone dormant, but hopefully some of the members would weigh in. I was looking forward to checking my website and reading their posts on what the clue could mean.

My brain needed a break. I shut down my iPad, opened my detective kit, and took out my fingerprinting materials. After picking out the clearest print in the dust on the windowsill, I covered it with a strip of clear tape and pressed it firmly down. I didn't have to brush on fingerprinting powder. The dust had done the job. I carefully peeled off the print and pasted it onto a Case Solution card.

Using my invisible marker I labeled it, "Turret Windowsill." Then I pulled out the box I had bought to hold fingerprints and clues, slipped my first Case Solution card inside, and closed the padlock. By the time the Skylar Robbins Detective Agency had solved its first big case, no doubt the box would be full.

Suddenly I heard a loud noise in the backyard and looked out my office window. Sledge was about to install our new rain gutters and I watched him for a minute. He walked through the side yard and out to the street, grabbing long sections of metal from the back of his truck. As he came back across the lawn his head swiveled back and forth, looking around. After he dumped the new rain gutters on the lawn in a big pile, he trotted back across the grass and stuck his head inside the greenhouse. Like he was searching for something. *Of course he was.*

I grabbed my pink Super-Zoom binoculars, turned off the light, and crouched down by the window to watch him. My binoculars rock. They were so strong I could see the hair on the back of his fingers as he picked up a section of metal half-pipe. A skuzzy blond guy picked up the other end, and they climbed up a couple of ladders and attached the new rain gutter to the house.

The hair on Sledge's arms was dark and curly.

Busted. I bet that *was* his hair that I found on my desk. So what was he doing in my office? There was no reason for him to be inside the house at all, unless he was looking for Xandra's clues. And what could I do about it?

Nothing. *Yet.*

My parents were totally impressed with Smack and his gang. I had to admit they were doing a great job remodeling our house. My mom was raving about them, even though she complained to my dad that they smelled "ripe," and she hated their snake and skull tattoos. I hated the fact that they were trying to find Xandra's jewels before I did.

But that wasn't going to happen. I hoped.

After dinner I had too much homework to work on clues, and started the problems on my algebra worksheet.

$72 = 9 \times B$

$550 \text{ km} = X \text{mm}$

$4A = 64$

$17.5 \text{ yards} = Z \text{ feet}$

I got a tingling feeling. In every equation, one thing stood for something else. I penciled in my answers with my brain ticking. The next section showed a bunch of different shapes, and asked whether or not they represented a polygon. I looked at each shape, circling *yes* or *no*. I finished the worksheet with my mind on something else. A similar problem, with a much more important solution: The squares on the third clue equaled—what?

My favorite detective show was about to start so I recorded it. Trying to forget about the mysterious clue, and the fact that a bunch of hostile men were right behind me in my search, I picked up my science book and read a chapter on anatomy. I put Mr. Bidden's signed permission slip into my backpack with a sinking feeling in my stomach.

12
Just Us Girls

The rest of the week flew by and before I knew it, it was Friday. I barely made it through lunch, I was so nervous about what would happen in Science. We had studied anatomy all week and I knew what was coming. My insides felt like I'd swallowed a grasshopper. Mr. Bidden collected our permission slips, making sure he got one from every single student. Then he passed out instruction sheets, smiling evilly at the class, showing off his long yellow teeth.

Dustin leaned toward me as we read the directions, and my heart flip-flopped. We were so close I could smell the fresh scent of his hair. Then Mr. Bidden passed out the dead frogs and I smelled something else. Something rank and rotting. Dustin took a plastic tray with a dead frog on it from the teacher, and I put my hand over my nose. The frog's skin looked rubbery and it really stunk. Cindy covered her mouth with one hand and leaned far back into her chair, staring at the frog with a horrified look on her face. Mark Oglethorpe gave Dustin a thin smile and said, "You go ahead."

"OK," Dustin agreed, "how about if I remove the organs, Skylar assists me, and you guys takes notes?" They both nodded their heads fast, relieved that they didn't have to touch any frog guts. Dustin looked at the little frog and picked up our scalpel. I hoped that when I assisted him our hands would brush past each other's and touch. Maybe he'd even let his rest against mine for a minute. *I wish!* Reality check: my fingers might land in rotten frog. I glanced at my anatomy notes and prayed I wouldn't throw up. My new cherry-scented lip gloss combined with the frog stench was making me sick to my stomach.

"Can you pull his legs apart a little?" Dustin asked, but I just sat there. "Don't worry, he won't bite you." He smiled at me with those straight white teeth and I melted.

The frog's tiny feet felt bony and sticky as I gently spread them apart. Dustin looked at me seriously, like a surgeon about to perform an operation. He sliced the dead frog down the middle and I recognized its heart, stomach, liver, and intestines from the diagrams I'd studied in my science book. The smell got stronger and I felt lunch rise up in my throat. "I'm sorry—" Dustin looked surprised when I suddenly screeched my chair back.

I bolted from the room and ran down the hall with Cindy Kowalski right behind me. Fortunately the bathroom was nearby. Shoving the door open, I slammed into a stall and knelt over the toilet bowl. Looking into the water, my face got sweaty and saliva filled my mouth. I spit into the toilet but I didn't throw up. Cindy retched into a toilet at the end of the row of stalls.

"Hey, are you guys OK?" a familiar voice asked.

I stood up and opened the door a crack. "Alexa?"

"Skylar?" We looked into each other's surprised faces.

"What are you doing in here in the middle of class?" she asked, frowning.

"Not ditching, if that's what you think. We were dissecting a frog and I almost barfed on Dustin."

Alexa burst out in a loud laugh and looked at the

floor. "I'm sorry. That's not funny," she said. Her lips were still twitching like she was holding back a giggle.

Cindy walked out of the stall and rinsed her mouth in the sink. She left the bathroom without looking at us.

"What about you?" I asked.

Alexa looked at me like she was trying not to smile. "I just started my period." It was her first time.

My mouth fell open. "You got it?"

"Just now. I totally just got it." Her cheeks turned pink and her eyes sparkled like she'd just opened the perfect Christmas present.

I took a step closer to her. "What happened?"

"I was sitting in class and my stomach started hurting again. I thought I had to go to the bathroom, so I got excused and came in here. When I pulled down my pants I realized I'd gotten it." Now Alexa smiled so wide I could see all of her teeth, right back to her molars.

"I'm so happy for you," I said, feeling more envious than happy.

"Me too. Except for starting it in school. Good thing I wasn't wearing white pants."

"I know, right? Who knows when I'll finally get mine." I looked down at the floor. "I'll probably need old lady diapers before I need tampons." My face got hot. I couldn't believe I was thirteen years old and had no clue when I would ever get my first period.

Alexa put her hands on her hips and looked at me like a mature girl who was giving advice to a little kid. "Stop it. You'll get it soon too."

My eyes started to water so I looked down and fished around in my purse, pulling out my lip gloss and putting some on. I needed to change the subject. "So did you have anything with you?"

"Yeah. My mom thought it was probably coming so she's been making me carry around a pad in my purse. She said all those stomach cramps I've been getting lately and my moodiness were probably PSM."

"What's PSM?"

"Pre-menstrual syndrome."

Oh. PMS.

"Good thing you had a pad." I didn't want to talk about Alexa's PMS anymore. Or the fact that she'd gotten her period and I still hadn't. "Come on," I said, shoving the door open. "We need to get back to class."

Alexa's mom gave me a ride home after school and I let myself into the empty house. Crew Gang had the day off while they waited for materials to come in, and for once our house didn't smell like B.O.

I was hungry and ate a package of peanut butter crackers without tasting them. Then I walked up the stairs to my bedroom. Heading over to my water quadrant, I sprinkled a little fish food into the bowl and watched my new black goldfish snap it up. I lit a stick of incense, and for some reason the sweet smell of vanilla made me feel sad. Climbing up to my office, I wandered over to the windowsill where I had found the fingerprint clue and looked down into the backyard. Maybe I would offer to help clean up the greenhouse this weekend so my mom could start to enjoy it. She'd been too busy writing history lectures to plant any flowers.

As soon as I thought of my mom I felt tears come to

my eyes and realized that I really needed to talk to her. Forcing myself to do homework for almost an hour, I finally heard the low grinding noise of the garage door opening far below me. Then I had to wait for her to come inside, set down her purse and briefcase, pee like she always had to after being stuck in traffic, and make a cup of tea. I sat on the top step of the first set of stairs with my chin in my hands until I heard the microwave ding, then walked downstairs and went into the kitchen.

"Hi Mom."

"Hi Honey." She took her cup out of the microwave, plopped in a tea bag, and dunked it up and down a few times. When she turned around and saw my face she walked over to me. "What's wrong? Is everything OK?" she asked, folding me into her arms. Then my mom pulled back so she could look me in the eye. "No, it's not," she answered herself as my eyes started to sting. "What happened today?" she asked, her hands still resting on my shoulders. I moved in for another hug.

"Alexa got her period," I mumbled into my mom's blouse. She tried to pull away to see my face but I didn't let go of her.

"And did that frighten her? Or you?" Then she stepped back and looked at me seriously.

This made me smile a little. "No, it wasn't scary or anything. It happened in class but she had a pad with her. She got cramps and thought she needed to go number two. It wasn't really a big deal."

"Let's sit down," my mom suggested, and we sat at the kitchen table. She blew across her tea and took a quiet sip, then looked into my eyes. "So, if it wasn't a big deal, why is it bothering you?"

I looked down, flicking the corner of the placemat. "Because I feel like a baby," I finally admitted. Knowing I'd feel like a really big baby if I started to cry, I couldn't manage to look at my mom after I said it. Just kept flicking the stupid placemat.

"Because Alexa got it before you did?" my mom asked, and I nodded without looking up. "Skylar, everyone matures at different rates. Like you had a growth spurt before Alexa and are taller than she is, and some of the other girls your age are taller than both of you. Just because you haven't gotten your period yet doesn't mean you won't get it soon. And even if you don't, it sure doesn't mean you're a baby."

Now I looked at her. "I sure feel like one. Cindy Kowalski's still twelve and she already uses the Kotex machine in the bathroom. I've seen her."

My mom smiled at me. "Well, periods can be crampy, and messy, and not very fun. But getting them *is* a mark of womanhood. How about this: be glad you don't have to deal with them for now. And when you *do* get it we'll do something fun, just the two of us, to celebrate. We'll slip away for secret sushi one night when your dad has his poker game. How 'bout that?"

The thought of a celebration made me smile. "I want him to go to secret sushi too," I said, thinking that the real secret would be that I'd gotten it.

"Deal," my mom agreed, reaching for my hand.

"Hey Mom, how about this weekend I'll help you clean up the greenhouse?" I suggested. Suddenly puttering around that musty old shed with my mom was the only thing I wanted to do.

"That sounds terrific," she said. "Just us girls." We looked at each other and nodded. I still felt envious that Alexa got it and I hadn't yet, but I sure felt a whole lot better.

13
Finding the Hidden Floor

Saturday I had to unpack boxes and load closets all morning, and after lunch my mom and I cleared all the dead plants out of the greenhouse and swept the floor. It wasn't exactly a party, but it kept me busy.

I was so excited about the first week at Pacific that I couldn't sit still while I waited for the weekend to be over. I had dissected a frog with Dustin Coles, who had picked *me* to be his partner! I couldn't wait to get back to class to see if he would pay attention to me again. All of my teachers were nice except creepy Mr. Bidden, and I liked all of my classes besides history. I had rubbed the smooth end of the lip gloss tube over my lips several times each day, and unless I was dissecting a frog, I loved it. I'd survived the embarrassing sweater incident, and it seemed like everyone had pretty much forgotten about it.

But there were some major things bothering me: Smack, Sledge, and Ignado snooping around our house trying to beat me to the jewels, and the fact that I couldn't decipher the mysterious drawing on the tattered yellow paper. After lunch I got back to work on the clue.

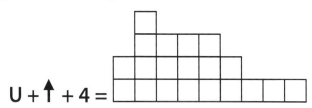

What could it mean? What did the squares stand for?

U + ↑ + 4 = 20 squares, so U + ↑ = 16 squares.

But if what if they weren't squares?

U + ↑ + 4 = X

Why couldn't I solve for X?

Picturing Grandpa stroking his chin and looking at me thoughtfully, I remembered something he used to say when he'd talk fondly about his partner. *Skylar, don't ever be afraid to ask for help if you can't figure something out or accomplish something by yourself. Sometimes two brains are better than one. Asking for backup does not mean you are weak, and refusing to accept help when you need it is just plain foolish.*

I logged onto my website and looked under *clues* to see what my secret agents had come up with. Five of them had posted some amazing guesses:

Water Nymph Agent # 003:
It means 8641 – it might be an address or a secret code number? Or maybe the amount each jewel is worth.

Fire Princess Agent # 005:
U = You
Arrow up = go up the blocks
Blocks = Houses
4 = Number of blocks
So you go up 4 blocks to find the jewels.

Shining Onyx Agent # 007:
You go up 4 times to find the next clue.

Thunder Cloud Agent # 004 and Roaring River Agent # 006:
You need to go up 4 levels for the jewels.

My agents were rocking the clues, but the information still seemed incomplete. I grabbed my cell, photographed the clue, and emailed it to Alexa with a message asking if she could help me decode it. She might not read very well, but she can look at a picture or a diagram and figure out what it means in seconds. Alexa always beats me at video games too; she can find her way out of a maze in a fraction of the time it takes me. And if I was going to find Xandra's jewelry box before Smack's crew did, I needed all the help I could get.

Before I could decide what to do next I heard the ear-splitting noise of Harleys ripping up our steep wind-ing hill. Flattening myself against the wall and peeking out my window, I looked toward the street. But I couldn't see anything beyond the side yard. Suddenly the bikes' motors stopped revving and the street went quiet. Then I heard the heavy crunching of boots on concrete.

Crew Gang was back.

But why? They didn't work on Saturdays.

They walked through the gate and marched toward the greenhouse. Grabbing my Soundtrap, I cracked my window open and pointed the thin microphone down toward the side of the yard they were heading for. First thing I heard after putting in my earbuds was Smack's squeaky voice barking orders. "Ignado! Pretend you're carrying these behind the shed, an' make a lot of noise dropping them so the dummies think you're busy doing somethin'. Then look inside that shed real good. There's 'apposed to be a clue to the fortune in there."

Hearing that felt like a punch in the stomach. I took out the earbuds and waited while pipes crashed noisily to the ground before I put them back in. *How do they know there's a clue in the greenhouse?!* I'd already searched it, *and* cleaned it with my mom, and I didn't find anything but dead plants, spider webs, and dirt. *Maybe they're just guessing. And who does he think he is, calling us* dummies?

Smack started to turn around so I flattened myself to the floor in case he looked up. I kept the microphone pointed toward them and the next voice I heard was Ignado's. "Ain't nothin' in that hothouse but junk. Let's get outta here." Turning off my Soundtrap, I got to my knees and watched them stomp across the driveway. Then motorcycles roared down our street and disappeared down the hill. They were here and gone within five minutes, marching in and out of our yard like they owned it.

Their visit proved that they were hunting for Xandra's jewels, and somehow they had information I didn't. I had even less time than I thought. And one less clue than I needed. I slipped the tattered paper into my pocket.

Flipping open my iPad cover, I read my detective notes. I was smarter than they were, and had to stick to my original plan. The clues would lead me in the right direction, and I would find what was hidden in the greenhouse if I followed them in the proper order.

There may be a hidden floor.
Hid her jewelry box somewhere on the estate.

Whoever is smart and brave enough to follow her clues inherits the jewels.
Find the dumbwaiter.

Locating the dumbwaiter would be my next goal. Running down the stairs, I decided to start searching on the first floor. The kitchen was the most logical place from which to lift meals, so that's where I began.

Both of my parents wanted to keep the antique fixtures, and except for a new dishwasher, garbage disposal, and refrigerator, the kitchen remained as it was a hundred years ago. Thin strips of wood called *crown molding* decorated the walls where they met the ceiling. A swirling design was carved into the wood, and the crown molding was stained with age. Faded wallpaper with delicate stripes had yellowed so much you could barely see the pattern. The sinks in the kitchen and the butler's pantry had old metal faucets with wing-shaped handles that squeaked when you turned them. All of the cupboards were narrow and had skinny doors. The mismatched handles were pitted with rust and dulled by tarnish. One of the handles was bolted in crooked, and my parents decided to leave it that way.

Shining my penlight into one corner of the kitchen, I got down on my hands and knees and peeked behind the cast iron stove. I ran my fingertips across the baseboards all around the room, searching for anything that was loose or strange in any way.

Nothing.

The room dimmed for a split second as if a shadow had passed by the small window. A chill crept through me. I felt like I was being watched. Had one of Smack's boys sneaked back into our yard to spy on me? One of them was so skinny his pants couldn't stay up. He had wispy yellow hair and pointy cheekbones that poked out of his face like wedges. More than once I'd turned around to find him *right* behind me. Smack had barked his name in front of me: Dusty. Judging by his sloppy clothes, greasy forehead, and grimy fingernails, his name should have been *Dirty*.

I twitched and looked up. The window was clear.

Shaking off the creepy feeling, I shined my light up at the ceiling, hoping for another hidden panel like the one I had found in the turret room cupboard. There wasn't one. The ceiling was solid. I let out a long hot breath.

I felt along the wall behind the oven, past the antique telephone that didn't work, and around the corner into the butler's pantry. That's where I stopped. Turning on my big flashlight, I shot the beam past the deep sink and the dishwasher, focusing on the locked door at the end of the room. That had to be where the dumbwaiter was. An idea hit me and I sprinted up the stairs to my parents' bedroom.

My mom was in the closet taking shoes out of a carton. "Hey, Mom? I searched all over the bottom floor and I can't find the dumbwaiter. Have you seen it up here?" On the far side of their bed was a sitting room. I wandered into it and looked around.

"It probably stops in the formal dining room. But I doubt if it works." She stuck her head back into the closet and started to unpack another box.

I ran down the hall and went into the big dining room,

and sure enough there was a narrow cupboard in one wall. The door squeaked when I opened it. *Sweet.* There was a metal contraption inside that looked like a rectangular box, open on the side that faced the door. On one edge a sticker read: **WEIGHT LIMIT: 150 POUNDS**.

Thick clamps were attached to the top and bottom of the box, with cables threaded through them that led to pulleys. A row of buttons next to the dumbwaiter was numbered 1, 2, 3, *and 4.*

This house does *have four floors,* I thought. *One of them* is *a hidden floor!*

"Can I see if it works?" I called.

"Sure, I guess," she said, bending over to open another box of shoes.

I pushed the button marked *3* and raced upstairs. *Way ahead of Smack's gang on this one.*

Ducking into the library down the hall from my bedroom, I ran up to the wall where I figured I would find the dumbwaiter. Sure enough, I spotted a narrow cupboard door. I heard a squeaking noise behind it and opened it up. Moments later the dumbwaiter creaked into view, stopping directly in front of the opening.

"Yes!"

Just like in the dining room, there was a row of buttons next to the dumbwaiter.

1, 2, 3, *4.*

I looked up at the ceiling. I thought about the house. My bedroom was on the third floor, and the turret room above it was the highest point on my side of the house. The little attic we used for storage was on the opposite end of the mansion. I remembered noticing the multilevel roof the first time we drove up the hill with Victoria Knight.

"Wait a minute!" I snatched the crumpled clue from my pocket and stared at it, remembering what my agents had posted: **You need to go up 4 levels for the jewels**. '

Suddenly the equation made perfect sense. U + ↑ + 4. "You plus up plus four," I breathed. I knew what I had to do. "I have to go up to four."

Racing into my bedroom, I grabbed my Porta-detective kit and ran back to the library. Ripping my penlight out of the kit, I stuck my head into the dumbwaiter and shined the beam all around. I couldn't see anything up or down the shaft past the metal sides of the box. Holding still, I listened hard until I was sure I didn't hear any footsteps on the stairs. My mom wasn't coming. The coast was clear.

I climbed into the dumbwaiter.

Nestling into the metal box, I pulled my feet inside and squirmed around until I was sitting cross-legged in the narrow space. No one much bigger than me would have been able to fit inside the dumbwaiter. Ms. Knight's words rang in my head: "Too small for a person to ride."

Unless that person was a skinny thirteen-year-old.

For a second I got very nervous, imagining all sorts of things that could go wrong. The metal cables holding the dumbwaiter up were old and might be rusty. They could snap in the middle of my ride and I would plunge down three stories, landing in a broken heap at the bottom of the elevator shaft. We could have a power failure and I could get stuck in the little metal box, trapped inside the wall. No one would know where I was or be able to find me. I could starve to death or die of thirst. While I starved to death, the rats that had nibbled the corners of the yellowed envelope could crawl inside the dumbwaiter and feast on me.

I took a deep breath and swallowed my fears. Finding another clue was way too important to chicken out. Reaching my arm outside of the little box, I hit the button marked *4* and ducked my head back inside.

The dumbwaiter started to rise.

Soon I was in pitch black, moving darkness, and my heart began to race. The dumbwaiter screeched and whined carrying my weight, and I started to panic. Turning on my penlight, I gritted my teeth to keep myself from crying out, when suddenly the little elevator slowed and stopped. A narrow door faced me, and I pushed it open and crawled through it.

The carpeted floor creaked beneath my feet as I took a careful step forward. The room was gloomy and painted with tall shadows. It stretched out ahead of me and disappeared around a bend. A little light came in through an air vent on one wall. Looking around with my heart hammering, my eyes finally adjusted to the dimness.

I was on the hidden floor!

I shined my penlight through the shadows. A soft throw rug lay at the foot of an elegant chair that was covered in midnight blue velvet. An old-fashioned floor lamp stood next to it and I turned the switch. It made a loud pop, and I flinched as the bulb lit briefly and burned out. A full-length mirror stood in front of me on a brass stand and my reflection startled me in the flash of light.

Turning around in a slow circle, I shined the narrow

penlight beam across the floor. "This was Xandra Collins's secret hideaway," I whispered. *Could her jewelry box be hidden up here?* I didn't have much time before my mom would notice I was missing. Or before Smack and the smelly boys figured out another way to get up here, right behind me.

The wall closest to me had a shelf bolted to it, full of books sandwiched between decorative bookends. I walked up to the shelf and shined my light on the spines so I could read some of the titles. *The Fine Art of Disguise and Other Parlor Tricks. Evading the Media. Into Thin Air.* I pulled the books forward and searched the area behind them. Nothing was hidden back there.

There was a brick fireplace in front of the elegant chair. I picked up the poker and dug through half-burned logs and ashes, hoping to find something buried beneath them, but there was nothing but soot. I turned to face the open part of the room, wishing I'd brought my jumbo flashlight with me.

There have to be clues up here!

Hurrying across the room, I aimed my penlight beam up and down the walls and over big oil paintings in heavy gold frames. Xandra Collins liked seascapes and moonlit forests. I peeked behind each painting, hoping to find a safe or a secret hiding spot. The walls behind them were solid. Blank. Empty.

Next I walked around a corner into another part of the floor. A sewing machine sat on a table with a little stool in front of it. Colorful bolts of fabric leaned against the wall. I ran my hand over a roll of purple velvet, sending a puff of dust into the air that made me sneeze. In the far end of the sewing area I saw a big pile of boxes, and shined my light on them.

I stared at the pile and a creepy feeling started to come over me.

Something familiar about all those boxes.

I counted them.

There were nine on the bottom row.

14
Trapped

My eyes widened. On top of the nine, there were more boxes. I nodded and quickly counted out loud. "One, two, three, four-five-six!" On top of the six boxes, there was another four. A big smile spread across my face. A final box rested on the top.

9 6 4 1. Now the symbol made sense, too.

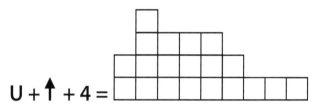

U + ↑ + 4 meant I had to go up four floors.

9 6 4 1 = 20 boxes. Stacked on the hidden floor.

I aimed my penlight's thin beam at the highest carton. Maybe Xandra Collins's jewelry box was hidden inside! Careful not to tumble the pile, I reached up and pulled down the box from the top of the stack. It was awfully light. Too light. I yanked the cardboard flaps apart.

White cotton stuffing filled the whole carton. I opened the box below it and found rolls of rickrack, bags of buttons and snaps, chalk for marking fabric, and a fat red pincushion. *Would all of the boxes be full of sewing supplies?* This stomped my enthusiasm for a minute, but then the detective in me took over and I remembered my Grandpa's words: *Look for clues in unexpected places.*

They won't be sitting right under your nose, waiting for you to find them. I pawed through one box after another like a dog trying to dig up a bone.

One box was full of newspaper clippings. I skimmed a few headlines but didn't read anything interesting. If only I had more time! The next carton contained an assortment of wigs, stage makeup, false beards and moustaches, and masks. Other boxes held a variety of costumes. Some were neatly folded and others were crumpled into balls and jammed into the boxes like they'd been hidden away in a hurry.

The second-to-last box was empty but it had something stuck to the bottom of it. I turned it upside down and banged on the cardboard. A warped photograph fluttered to the floor. I picked it up and shined my penlight on it. The picture was of a beautiful lady with slightly tilted, almond-shaped eyes and a small smile on her face. She looked happy and full of mischief at the same time. Long black hair streaked in silver hung way past her shoulders. She wore a dazzling diamond necklace around her neck.

"Xandra Collins," I whispered. "It has to be." Putting the picture in my back pocket, I opened the last box and let out a quiet whoop. A torn piece of paper with mysterious writing on it was taped to the bottom and I peeled it off. Shining my penlight on the paper, I saw some half circles, lines, and a bunch of little numbered footprints drawn with a fine-point, black felt-tipped pen. About a third of the page was missing.

The fourth clue.

The footprints on the paper were totally random, like

a picture of the snow after someone had walked around in it. "Dance steps?" I decided to go downstairs where I would have plenty of light and room to move around so I could follow the footsteps. Folding the paper carefully, I tucked it into my bra so it would be hidden in case I ran into any of the construction workers when I got back downstairs.

I took one last lap around the hidden floor, shining my light into the corners, wondering if I had missed anything important and wishing I had more time to explore. "There could be clues hidden between the pages of those books, and those articles could be important," I muttered, hurrying back over to the messy piles of boxes I'd rummaged through. The second I bent over for a closer look, I bolted back and gasped. A dead scorpion was stuck to the corner of the top box like she had been pasted there on purpose. Her pointy pincers curled up over her brittle, dry spine.

Was this a threat? Or just a random dead arachnid?

Don't be stupid, I thought. There were more dead bugs, spiders, and even lizards than I could count when we first saw the house. This was just another one—nothing more. Or was it? No time to worry about it now. I piled the boxes back up in the same arrangement I'd found them: 9 6 4 1.

Trying to forget about the scorpion, I continued my search and found a narrow door at the dark end of the sewing area. After walking up to it and pulling it open, I aimed my penlight down a steep flight of shadowy stairs. *This must be how Xandra got up here!*

I hurried down the narrow staircase, and when I hit

the last step I was in front of another door. It was locked from my side, so I unlocked the handle and turned it. A solid panel faced me. "That's why her heirs never found the hidden floor," I said, touching the rough wood and wondering what was on the other side. "There must be a button somewhere that moves the panel so you can access the secret staircase." I left the door unlocked so if I found the button I could come back to this floor without riding the dumbwaiter. Hopefully Crew Gang wouldn't find it before I did. After climbing back up the stairs I took a last look around, then crawled back into the little elevator.

I punched *1* and the dumbwaiter started to move. I wondered where it would stop, and where in the house I would come out. The black box creaked slowly down through the floors. Fortunately Xandra Collins's heirs and the construction workers were too big to fit into the dumbwaiter. Otherwise they might have discovered the hidden floor and found the fourth clue. When the dumbwaiter finally hit the bottom, I was staring at the inside of yet another door. I pushed it, but it wouldn't open.

"So that's why I couldn't find the dumbwaiter on the bottom floor," I said to myself. "It *is* behind the locked door in the butler's pantry."

And then I panicked. How was I supposed to make the elevator move up to the second story so I could get out? The box was dark and there was no way to reach outside of it to push the buttons to change floors.

I slapped my hands against the door as hard as I could. Then I really banged my fists against it while I tried not to scream.

I was trapped inside the dumbwaiter.

15
Escape

Just as I was about to start shouting for help, I stopped myself. Not only would I get in huge trouble if my mom caught me riding the dumbwaiter, but we didn't have a key to unlock this door anyway. My heart pounded. There was no way to get back up to the other floors by using the dumbwaiter, since there was nothing outside of it but a locked door where the keypad should have been. It could be days before anyone found me. I could suffocate or die of thirst!

"Calm down and use your brain," I said out loud. The dumbwaiter was so stuffy I smelled my own breath. There wasn't much time before I ran out of air.

Look for clues on the floor, all four walls, and the ceiling.

I felt the inside of the dumbwaiter quickly, one wall at a time from top to bottom, like a mime doing, "trapped in a box." My heart hammered and I was ready to cry. I dragged my fingers back and forth across the ceiling and up and down the walls, searching desperately for a way out. The walls were smooth and I was definitely stuck.

After aiming my penlight beam all around, I finally spotted a little red button in the upper right-hand corner of the ceiling. It wasn't marked. I didn't have a choice. I pushed it.

Slowly, the dumbwaiter started to climb.

I held my breath as I felt myself moving upward, and then the little elevator made a grinding noise and stopped. Inching the narrow door open to just a crack, I looked into the formal dining room. My mom was around the corner, humming to herself. I couldn't get out of the dumbwaiter here! Quietly I pulled the cupboard door closed and pushed the emergency button again. If she heard the sound of the dumbwaiter, hopefully she would think I was just playing with it, not riding it.

Up I went, climbing out of the stuffy box and into the library. Then I hurried down the hall to my room, shaking so hard I could barely walk. After lying down on my bed until my heart stopped pounding, I sat up and looked at the footsteps on the clue, then decided to follow the footstep pattern.

"One, two, three," I said, staring at the paper and stumbling around, "four—wait a minute. Where's five six and seven?" I stopped in my tracks as I heard my mom coming up the stairs. The clue was a dead giveaway that I was looking for the jewels, so I put it in my pocket and held my breath until she passed my room, continuing down the hall.

I wanted to make my dad proud of my investigation, and make my mom realize that taking risks was worthwhile. Smack's crew was not going to find the jewels before I did. I wanted to rub my hands together in satisfaction and say, "Case *closed*," like my grandfather. I needed to find Xandra's jewelry box before my parents figured out what I was doing and forced me to stop, since they would have thought it was way too dangerous.

As it turned out, they would have been right.

16
Dusting for Fingerprints

Peeking into the hall, I watched my mom until she disappeared into the library. Then I crept up the spiral staircase into my office, shutting the door. I looked at the paper containing the clue under my magnifying glass. It didn't look any different, just bigger. I opened my iPad cover.

After typing in the numbers inside the footprints, I looked at the result: 1 2 3 4   1 2 3   1 2 3 4 5 6   1 2 3 4 5   1 2 3   1 2 3 4   1 2 3   1 2 3 4 5 6. Without the other symbols, the numbers made even less sense than they did on the clue. I got up and tried to follow the footprint map inside my office but I just got dizzy walking around in circles. If these were dance steps, this was the dumbest dance anybody ever did.

I decided to make a list of the case notes and clues I had found so far.

1. Three years ago Xandra Collins mysteriously disappeared. She may have been kidnapped.
2. She left clues to find her hidden jewelry box.
3. Her heirs searched for three years and didn't find them. (They didn't look hard enough.)
4. The first clue was fingerprints on the turret room windowsill, leading to the cupboard. (Clue #1)
5. The cupboard had a note written on the wall in invisible ink: Things in this room are not always what they seem. (Clue #2)
6. The top of the cupboard was phony. Taped

above the false ceiling was an old envelope. Inside was a piece of paper with a square design on it. (Clue #3)
7. The squares stood for boxes.
8. The boxes were stacked on the hidden floor. You have to squeeze inside the dumbwaiter or climb up a secret staircase to find it. This may be why her heirs never did. They weren't small enough, smart enough, or brave enough.
9. A picture of Xandra Collins was inside the second-to-last box.
10. The box below that one contained a paper with numbered footprints on it. Some of the footprints are missing. There are half-circles and a rectangle among the footprints. (Clue #4)

I took the picture of Xandra Collins out of my pocket and stared at it. She stared back at me with a curious smile, like she was trying to tell me something. But what? When I turned it over to look at the back of the photo, I couldn't believe my eyes. On the back of the picture of the mysterious woman, someone had written a big *X*.

X for Xandra?

X marks the spot?

X her out?

Who had written the *X*?

I dropped the picture like a hot potato. Suddenly I couldn't get it out of my fingers fast enough. "Stupid!" I scolded myself, hoping that if there were prints on the picture I hadn't smeared them or covered them with my own.

Trace evidence.

I opened my detective kit and took out my dusting powder and brush. Picking up the photo with tweezers, I examined the edges. They were light, so I chose the black fingerprint powder. When I dusted it carefully over the edges using my big soft brush, I saw nice juicy prints on both sides. And they were too big to be mine. After blowing off the excess powder I pressed down a clear piece of tape, lifted the cleanest print, and pasted it onto a Case Solution card. Using my invisible ink marker, I labeled this one, "Print on Xandra's picture."

The metal box I had bought for collecting clues was inside the deep drawer in the bottom of my desk. I unlocked my clue box and took out the Case Solution card containing the fingerprint from the windowsill, then compared the prints under my magnifying glass. *They matched.* Both of the prints were Xandra's. The first piece of the puzzle had just snapped into place. I stared out the window across the hills at the hazy blue of the distant ocean, thinking. Then I put the two Case Solution cards, the footprint map, the box design clue, and Xandra's picture back inside the box and locked it. "Now what?" I asked myself.

My notes ended in a big puzzle. The clues helped me find a map that had numbered footsteps on it, but a chunk of it was missing. Xandra had written an *X* on the back of her picture. Why? This was where the information ended. I turned off my iPad and walked down the spiral staircase to my bedroom. Lying down on my bed, I closed my eyes, my mind spinning with secret codes, unanswered questions, and the puzzling map.

17
The Map with the Missing Footsteps

When I got home from school Monday I walked through the front door and came face-to-face with Ignado. He stood aside like he was allowing me to enter my own home, staring at me with his brown eye while the blue-gray one veered off to one side. He tossed his screwdriver up in the air over and over, catching it one-handed, while he eyeballed me. Our living room smelled like sweet sawdust and harsh sweat.

"Excuse me," I said, trying to brush past him.

"No. You wait a minute," he said, grabbing my arm with a calloused hand. My heart lurched. No one his age had ever threatened me before. The skin on Ignado's cheeks was pitted with acne scars. His brown hair was separated into greasy hanks. He flipped a few of them over his left shoulder as he leaned toward me, reeking of cigarettes.

I pretended I was checking out the remodel as I looked around, hoping to spot my mom. She had a short day on Mondays, but didn't always come right home after work. My dad was working in his lab, but there was so much construction noise he probably wouldn't hear me unless I screamed as loud as I could. I tried to swallow, but my throat wasn't working. "Um, what?" I stammered.

Ignado's brown eye jittered as he glanced from one side of the room to the other, probably wondering if either of my parents were nearby. Then he stared at me hard and smirked. "Why'd you need my screwdriver for? When I borrowed it to you the other day."

Feeling my hands bunching up by my sides, I forced myself to relax. Wouldn't do any good to let him know he was scaring me. "Because I needed to hang a picture," I fibbed. "In my room."

"Well, I been in your room. An' there ain't no pictures hangin' up there." Ignado smiled and folded his arms, like he'd caught me in a lie. Proud of himself. He leaned toward me and his brown eye narrowed. "And I saw your kit, *Little Miss Detective*." He spit out the words like he'd bitten into a raw onion. Glaring at me.

When I get scared I think of my grandfather telling me never to back down when I'm in the right. So I took a step closer. So close I could smell his dirty hair. "Well, I figured you wouldn't know what a *Dream Catcher* was, so I called it a 'picture.' You know that wooden circle with yarn woven through it, decorated with seashells? That's what I needed to screw into the wall." I took a deep breath, hoping he hadn't noticed I'd hung it with a nail, not a screw. "And, why were you in my room? There weren't any curtains to hang up there."

Ignado's pale, cloudy eye didn't close all the way when he blinked. The hand that wasn't holding the screwdriver clenched into a fist. "Just checking on the remodel." He glared at me. I noticed little balls of perspiration beading up on his forehead.

"OK. Sure," I muttered.

"Don't be stupid," he warned.

Maybe I'd better start playing stupid, I thought, *so they don't think I'm a threat.* "Huh?" I asked, like I had no idea what he was talking about.

"Nuthin'."

I shrugged, brushed past him, and headed upstairs with my heart pounding.

My mom's voice stopped me from the bottom of the first set of steps. I'd never been so glad to hear it in my life. "Skylar, hurry up. It's after three."

"Hurry up and what?" I asked, looking down the staircase at her.

"Ballet day, remember?" she called. I'd completely forgotten. Like I could even think about dancing around in my pink tights when there was a bunch of stinky bikers trying to find Xandra's jewels before I did, threatening me inside my own house.

"Mom, I'm sick of ballet." I got to the top of the second staircase and hurried into my room, out of sight of the construction creeps. My mom clomped up the stairs and came into my bedroom, looking annoyed. I whirled around, thinking fast. "It's so boring compared to gymnasti—"

"Skylar." She interrupted me, sticking out her index finger. I knew she was about to count something up to prove her point. "We just bought you new ballet shoes and tights." Her first finger stood for the expense of my shoes and tights. "And money doesn't grow on trees around here." She looked at me to make sure I was paying attention before she touched her middle finger. "We pay in advance each month and you have prepaid lessons to take. We can't afford to waste money since we just bought this huge new house that you and your father insisted on."

That *we* insisted on. Nice. "OK, I'll pay you back for the lessons. I'm sick of bal—"

She wasn't finished. Her ring finger was next. "You said you wanted to take ballet for another year and—"

"And I changed my mind. I'm tired of it now. It's boring and I hate the music." *And I have clues to find!*

My mom talked right over me. "—when you make a *commitment*, you stick to it."

"I have homework." *And I need to find the next clue before Crew Gang does. Ignado called me,* Little Miss Detective. *They obviously know I'm looking for the hidden jewels too.*

"You can do it after dinner. Now hurry up and get ready." She clip-clopped down the stairs and I grabbed my head in my hands. *I can't leave the house while Crew Gang is here!* I wanted to tell my mom so badly that the construction workers were threatening me. Trying to beat me to Xandra's jewels. But I couldn't say a word if I wanted to find them first. My mom was always warning me not to do anything dangerous. Like she'd ever let me compete with Smack's crew for a gazillion dollars worth of diamonds. I'd be grounded before I could even say "jewelry box." I didn't have a choice. After I changed into my ballet clothes, I ran downstairs and headed for the garage.

One brown eye followed me all the way to the door.

That night I called Alexa and told her all about the hidden floor, and then I studied algebra until bedtime. It took me a really long time to fall asleep, and when I finally did I had a strange dream: Wearing my ballet shoes, tights, and a leotard, I slipped outside into the pitch-black backyard and walked around blindly with my arms out in front of me. Screwdrivers, hammers, and nails stuck up out of the grass and I tried not to step on them, taking small, mincing steps. I searched for something while I tried to avoid stumbling over the railing and plunging into the canyon. The ragged mountainside beckoned me. I crept closer. There was a clue that I needed to find, and I ignored the danger of the cliff. Feeling along the cold metal railing, I reached the end and then turned around. After doing *grand jetes* toward the center of the yard, I did *pirouettes* until I got dizzy and fell onto my back on the grass. Then I sat up and tried to focus my eyes in the dark.

I was looking at the gazebo.

The next morning I woke up groggy. I hadn't slept well, and the mysterious meaning of my dream was nagging at me. A force had pulled me into the backyard. Like there was a clue that was demanding to be found. By me.

I crawled out of bed and climbed the spiral stairs to my office. Sitting down at my desk, I unlocked my clue box and took out the picture of Xandra Collins. Her eyes twinkled like she had a secret to tell. "Where did you hide the next clue?" I whispered. "And what does the map with the missing footsteps mean?" Xandra smiled her mysterious smile, but her tilting eyes didn't give up any answers. The memory of the dream tapped at my brain like a woodpecker, letting me know it was something I needed to pay attention to.

After deciding to re-create my dream, I hurried out

into the backyard and walked slowly toward the metal fence, skipping the ballet moves. Wisps of fog swirled around the hills, moving in and around the peaks like floating ghosts. The grass was damp with dew, smelling fresh and green in the thin morning sun. Hanging onto the first section of railing, I bent over it and looked down into the steep canyon. Jagged rocks jutted out of the hillside. Yellow, orange, and red nasturtiums and wild mustard weeds grew in between the boulders. The mustard plants had tiny yellow blossoms and bright green leaves with wavy edges.

I followed the guardrail all around the side of the backyard until it ended near the greenhouse. Then, as I had in my dream, I wandered into the center of the yard and twirled around until I got dizzy before I collapsed onto my back on the grass.

The sky continued to spin above me. When it stopped moving and I sat up, the gazebo was in front of me. I got a funny tingling feeling, like I had done this all before. The gazebo was still covered in peeling white paint, and the bench had the same stained cushions on it from before we moved in. My mom had been too busy grading history essays and writing lectures to fix it up. I walked inside and sat on the bench.

At first I didn't notice anything. Then my eyes traveled up to the highest peak: the pointy tip that matched the ceiling in my office. I remembered noticing a bird's nest up there the first time Ms. Knight showed us the gazebo. The same nest was balanced up on the rafter, so I climbed up onto the table to see if it held any eggs. It was empty, dry, and dusty. Some crafty bird had woven pine needles and dry twigs together in a nice tight circle and lined the nest with torn pieces of white paper topped with dead grass. I stood on my tiptoes for a better look and grabbed the rafter to steady myself. And my heart skipped a beat.

On one of the pieces of paper there were some faint, numbered footprints.

My pink sneakers wobbled on the tabletop. *It's part of the map! One of those pigeons must have found this tucked away somewhere when the house was abandoned and used it for her nest. This is what my dream was trying to tell me: Look in the bird's nest.*

Then I heard Smack's squeaky voice shouting from across the lawn. It got louder as he came closer to where I was hiding. I jumped off the table and ducked, flattening myself onto the ground. Slowly inching forward, I peeked through the slats in the gazebo. "This is all you got, Dummy? I tole you to order ten percent more than you needed, Dusty. Now we gotta go to Home Depot." Smack cussed loudly and spat a thick loogey onto our grass. Dusty stomped back to the pickup truck with Smack following on his short legs, grumbling about the extra cost. Fortunately they were so busy arguing that they hadn't spotted me. I stayed on my stomach with my heart pounding until I heard their truck rumble down the hill, and then I climbed shakily to my feet.

Looking back into the nest, I thought about all of the places we'd seen bird turds before we moved in. Pigeons had roosted all throughout the house. There was part of a nest in what became my mom's sitting room. Bird droppings littered the floor of the butler's pantry, the library, and the garage. Wherever Xandra had hidden the other half of the map, some clever bird had found it and used it to pad her nest. *And I found it before Crew Gang did.*

Reaching up, I pulled the bird's nest down and set it gently on the table. Then I carefully lifted out three soft pieces of dirty paper. They were stained and a little bit shredded, but I could still make out numbered footsteps and shapes on them. After replacing the bird's nest on the rafter, I picked up the fragile pile and cradled it between my hands while I raced upstairs to my office.

Sitting down at my desk, I unlocked my clue box and took out the partial map from the hidden floor, smoothing it out in front of me:

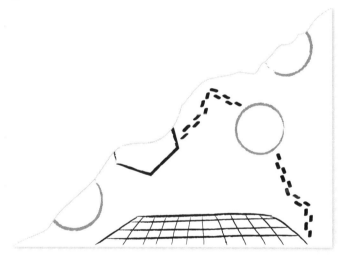

I set the first torn piece of bird's nest paper next to it. "Wait a minute," I said aloud, picking up another piece. *The footprints on the bird's nest paper had the missing numbers on them.* There were also some curving shapes on the strips that looked like C's and other marks that looked like L's. I rearranged the papers until C-shapes met each other and formed whole circles, the L's combined to form a hexagon, and all of the footprints flowed in numerical order. Then I carefully taped the map together. There was still a chunk of it missing.

After the final footprint there was an *X*. The same curved *X* that was written on the back of Xandra's picture.

X marks the spot.

Now I just have to figure out where to take footstep number one.

The fragile bird's nest papers teased me. *Where did the map start, and what did the symbols on it mean?* I was having trouble figuring it out by myself. I needed backup, and looked forward to talking it over with Alexa.

I picked up Xandra Collins's picture and smiled at her. She smiled back, as if she knew I was starting to figure out her clues.

18
The Threat

The next morning before breakfast I went into the bathroom to brush my teeth and take a shower. Something stunk. Bad. No one used this bathroom except me, and I hadn't gone yet. But something *reeked*. Maybe one of our hundred-year-old pipes was leaking and something was rotting. I stepped into the shower and tried to ignore the stench. My dad and the construction crew would have to figure out what was stinking and fix it.

While I blow-dried my hair, I tried to decide which shoes to wear. Ugh, something really smelled. Looking forward to science class when I'd see Dustin again, I figured I'd put on a little eye shadow. I pulled out the center drawer, where I kept my makeup.

Ignado's threat suddenly became crystal clear. A pile of what looked like rat turds were sprinkled across the back of my hand mirror and squished on the cover of my eye shadow. There was a nasty brown streak on the cover of my lip gloss. Definitely some kind of poop. There were no stray animal hairs or paw prints, just piles of rodent dung plopped on my mirror and smeared on my makeup. *Maybe a rat didn't leave these,* I thought. *Maybe a human put them there on purpose.* I could picture Smack, hands on his hips, legs bowed, smirking at me. But that couldn't be what was smelling up my bathroom. There were only a few turds and smears fouling up my makeup drawer.

I whirled around and looked out the open door and

down the hall. No one was there. Taking a quick breath, my eyes darted into every corner of the bathroom. I expected rats to pop out and bite me at any second. The back of my neck prickled. Nothing moved. I needed my detective tools and rushed back into my room, grabbing my Porta-detective kit. Armed with my fingerprinting materials, mini-mag glass, and an evidence envelope, I ran back into the bathroom and pulled on a pair of latex gloves, snapping them tightly against my wrists.

I opened the drawer on the right side of the vanity, pulling it all the way out. All it contained was my brushes, combs, a curling iron, and my blow drier. No clues, but I planned to dust it for fingerprints.

Then I opened the left-hand drawer. And lurched backward, putting my hand over my mouth while I tried not to throw up. I saw its tail first.

Nestled in the back corner was a putrid, decaying rat. Its rancid guts spilled over the edges of its split gray skin like pudding. I bent over, clutched my stomach, and dry heaved. The stench was horrible. I had to get rid of it, but there was no way any particle of dead rat was touching me. I could barely stand to look at it. Grabbing a trashcan liner from the cupboard below the sink, I wrapped it around my hand. Leaned away from the drawer and glanced at the soft, dead rodent, so disgusted I was ready to throw up. I couldn't actually pick up a dead animal, *could I?*

Then I pictured Smack and Ignado, smirking at me, calling me, "Little Miss Detective". I was stronger than they were. I could do this. I *would* do this. That was my motto. Taking a deep breath, I reached my hand forward with the trash bag wrapped around my fingers. *Ugh*! Picked up the squishy, bloated morsel by its stiff, skinny tail, and with one quick motion I flipped it into the plastic bag. Spun the bag around to seal it up and then closed it with a twist tie. I couldn't wait to let go of it, and flung it onto the floor by the door. Then I stepped into the tub, reached up and opened the window to let the smell out.

I looked back into my makeup drawer. A few stray rat hairs littered the bottom. Besides the hairs and the poop smeared on my cosmetics, there were no clues. When I got home from school I could clean it out and wash my mascara and eye shadow with anti-bacterial soap. Or maybe throw them out and buy new ones. I'd have to completely disinfect the left-hand drawer.

Resting my hands on the new granite countertop, I closed my eyes and tried to hold my breath while I thought about the dead rat. It was definitely a message. Maybe Smack knew that I was sneaking around behind my parents' backs, hoping they wouldn't find out I was looking for the jewels. His workers were in our house constantly, snooping. Every time I turned around, Dusty, that lint-thin creep with the yellow hair, was staring at me. Probably overheard every argument I'd had with my mom. She was obviously overprotective, and Smack's crew had been all up in our stuff for weeks. They had to know I wouldn't tell my parents that we were competing for a million dollar prize or I'd get myself in big trouble. And that made me really mad.

As soon as I got mad, I started to feel better. Stronger. Back in control.

What did they think they could do to me when my

parents were paying them and my dad was right downstairs working in his lab? Booby-trap something?

Suddenly it felt like the floor shifted beneath me as if I was about to black out. *Maybe that's why the dumbwaiter got to the bottom floor and stopped behind the locked door!* Had Smack or Ignado rigged the dumbwaiter knowing I'd ride it to find the hidden floor? Were they right behind me, following Xandra's clues?

No. Not possible.

They could have used their tools to break through our walls and get to the hidden floor if they knew that's where I was headed, or if they knew that's where the next clue was hidden. They were putting up new drywall all over the place. It would have been way too easy for them to cover their tracks. Smack's crew had access to our whole house and every tool imaginable. So they must have known I was one step ahead of them. Which was why they were trying to frighten me with stupid threats.

Although to be honest, the dead rat had me completely freaked. Not only had they planted it in my bathroom and smeared my makeup with poop when no one was looking, they knew me well enough to realize I wouldn't tell my parents that they were sending me a warning.

Time to ditch the evidence. Picking up the rat bag, I ran down two flights of stairs as fast as I could and ducked into the garage, dumping the bag into a garbage can. When I walked back into the house my spine tingled. I turned around and sure enough Ignado was leaning against one wall, staring at me with one, unblinking eye.

"Hi, Ignado," I said, folding my arms. I stood perfectly still and looked at him calmly. "All done working in my *bathroom?*"

He said nothing. Just turned around and fussed nervously with a paint pan. *Busted*. I'd won this round, and Ignado knew it.

But the game was far from over.

19
Bird's Nest Clue

There was no time to talk to Alexa during class and tell her what was going on. At lunch, we walked down the cafeteria aisle, taking icky entrees from under the warming lamps and putting them on our trays. I passed greasy cardboard bowls of macaroni and cheese that looked dry and dark on top and picked up a wrinkled hot dog. It looked like a science experiment from Mr. Bidden's class. "I don't know why I begged my mom to let me buy my lunch," I said. "This stuff is gross."

"But bringing a sack lunch is so *elementary school.* At least the salads look OK."

We dug money out of our purses and paid, while the kids behind us racked metal trays forward, rushing us out of the line. Stepping into the fresh air, we looked around for a seat at a cool table. I spotted Dustin eating with Brendan. Alexa saw an open space across from them and elbowed me.

"No way. I'm not just going over there and sitting with him," I whispered.

"Have it your way," Alexa said, as Emelyn Peters and her friends pounced on the open bench across from Dustin and the other cutest guys in school. Emelyn's loud giggles echoed across the quad. Glancing back into the covered area, I checked out the other popular table. The guys were eating and the girls were texting while they glanced around to see if anyone was looking at them.

"Ugh," I said. "Let's go sit on the lawn."

We sat down cross-legged and rested our trays on our laps. I took a bite of the salty hot dog. It tasted a lot better than it looked. "So how's the treasure hunt going?" Alexa asked, leaning forward with her dimples showing.

I ran my hand over the scratchy grass, its roughness tickling my palm. "Glad you asked, because I need your help." I looked up at her, smiling. "I found pieces of a map inside a bird's nest in the gazebo. They were part of the map I found on the hidden floor."

"A bird's nest?" Alexa stopped chewing and looked at me. "How'd you think to look in there?"

"I had this weird dream about the gazebo so I decided to search it," I said, wrapping a strand of hair behind my ear. "When we first looked at the house, I saw a bird's nest up in the rafters. It was made of twigs and pine needles, and lined with pieces of dirty white paper. Those slips of paper must have stuck in my brain, and the dream reminded me to look at them. When I investigated the nest I saw footprints drawn on the papers. They matched the ones on the partial map I found."

Alexa shook her head. "You're amazing. Now what?"

I swallowed. "That's the problem. The map shows how many paces to go in different directions, but it doesn't tell where to begin." I looked at Alexa, scrunching my napkin into a little ball.

She guessed what I was thinking and her eyes widened. "Maybe I can help you figure out where to start."

"I was hoping you'd say that," I said.

Alexa is way better than I am at seeing where things are in relation to each other and how things fit together. She loves puttering around in my dad's gadget room, and figured out how the remote controls for our television and DVR worked without anyone even having to explain them. Alexa can find her way around a new neighborhood much better than I can. I always follow her when we explore on our bikes because I'd probably get us lost.

"I have something else to tell you." The hair on the back of my neck prickled when I thought about it.

"What?" Alexa asked. The freckles stood out on her cheeks.

"The construction crew remodeling our house? They're looking for the jewels too."

Alexa looked at me and the hand holding her fork dropped into her lap. "No way."

"Yes. I've caught them snooping more than once. And one of them—" I looked away. Didn't want to say it.

Alexa stopped chewing. "Go on."

"Seemed like he was—threatening me, almost."

"No way," Alexa whispered, so intensely it almost seemed like she'd shouted. "How?"

"He loaned me his screwdriver, and then he totally grilled me about what I used it for when I gave it back."

Alexa's forehead wrinkled as she thought about it. "That's not so bad, really." She stared at me. "Something else must have happened."

I didn't want to tell her, but I had to. "This morning I found rat turds in my makeup drawer."

"Maybe you have rats," Alexa said, sensibly. When she saw my expression, her face fell. "It wasn't rats?"

"Well, there was rat poop all over the place when we moved in. But I think this particular poop was put in my bathroom drawer on purpose. There were little piles mounded on my mirror and smeared on my makeup, but very little anywhere else."

"Maybe it was a very neat rat." Alexa smiled.

"Very funny."

"Sorry."

"I think it was Smack's guys trying to send me a message." I glanced up at Alexa. My throat went dry, remembering it.

She stopped eating and looked at me. "Go on."

I took a drink. "This morning. In the back of one of my other drawers—"

"What, Skylar?" She knew me well enough to figure out that there was something horrible coming. Something I was afraid to tell her. Her face paled. "Tell me."

My mouth felt chalky as I remembered the smell. I set down the end of the hot dog, sure if I took another bite I'd throw up. "Squished in the corner there was a dead rat. Really dead. Like split open, reeking dead."

Alexa covered her mouth with both hands. Her eyes went so wide I could see white all the way around the green parts. "Gross! Are you serious?"

"Completely. I think it was a threat. It's like Smack's gang knows I'm searching for the jewels too and they're trying to scare me off so they can beat me to it. And they are *not* going to beat me to it."

"Skylar," She leaned forward and grabbed my arm. "They killed a rat?"

"No, they must have found it. That one had been dead for a *while*."

"Still, that's so scary. You better not do anything—"

"What," I interrupted. "Dangerous?" She sounded

123

just like my mom. "This could be exactly what my detective agency needs. It doesn't even have 200 Likes on Facebook and I'm barely getting any shares. If I find Xandra's jewels before anyone else, do you realize how huge that could be?" I looked at Alexa like she was crazy for not understanding, and she looked at me like I was being a complete fool.

"God, Skylar, just be careful for once. OK?"

"What are you, my mom?" I hated it when people told me to be careful. That bugged me more than anything, and my BFF should have known it. Alexa's cheeks turned pink. "Sorry, Lex. I just hate that a bunch of stupid guys are snooping around my house, giving me these looks like they own the place. Well they are not finding Xandra's jewelry box before I am, not matter what."

Alexa shook her head but didn't comment. Dustin and his friends got up from their table and walked past us across the lawn, shouting and laughing. "There goes Brendan," I said, and Alexa followed him with her eyes.

"So has Dustin talked to you?" she asked, obviously happy to change the subject.

"Not really." I took a sip of my drink. "After anatomy Mr. Bidden made us all switch seats so we would work with different partners. Dustin said *hi* to me once. That's it."

"At least you got to sit next to him and do a lab together. Brendan hasn't even looked at me." Brendan hurried ahead of Dustin and his friends and turned around, gesturing wildly, making everyone laugh. Alexa stared at him for a minute. "Do you think he might go to the dance with me?"

"What dance?"

"*What dance?*" Her light eyebrows climbed up her forehead. "Are you kidding me?" I shook my head. "There's a big dance coming up with a live band. I saw a poster in the hall this morning, and everyone was talking about it in ceramics."

"When?" I asked, looking around for proof of some big dance. "And you think Brendan and Dustin would actually ask us?"

Alexa shook her head. "It's in like three weeks. And they couldn't even if they wanted to. It's a backwards dance."

"What does that mean? Wait—we have to ask them?" Total nightmare. "No way."

"Yes," Alexa nodded. "I don't know about you, but I'm asking Brendan before someone else does. You should too," she said, as Emelyn and her friends got up from their table and hurried to catch up with Dustin and Brendan. Emelyn swished white-blonde hair over her shoulder and giggled so loudly we could hear it from across the lawn.

"I guess," I said quietly, picking at my napkin.

"Come on don't be scared." Alexa looked at me with a challenging smile. "He's had a crush on you since fifth grade."

I looked at her like she had to be kidding. "No he hasn't. Don't you remember in elementary school whenever he saw an *A* on my papers he'd say in that voice like I was a total joke, 'Oh of *course* Skylar got another *A*'?"

Alexa looked at me like she couldn't believe I didn't get this. "You just didn't realize when he teased you it meant he was interested. Why do you think Emelyn hates you so much? She's always been jealous."

"*She's* been jealous of *me*? No way."

"She has *so* been jealous of you. And you'll see why. Dustin's going to say *yes*. As soon as you ask him." Alexa nodded confidently.

I got a sinking feeling. Took a deep breath and blew it out. The backwards dance was only a few weeks away. And I had science class with Dustin next period.

20
Could Dustin Coles Actually Like Me?

he next morning I woke up before my alarm went off. Xandra's treasure map and Smack's crew were the last things on my mind. I had chickened out after lunch, but Alexa convinced me to ask Dustin to go to the dance with me the next chance I got. My stomach felt like it had a toad leaping around in it every time I thought about it.

After jumping into the shower and washing my hair, I blew it dry upside down to make it full and pinned the sides up in some sparkly pink barrettes. I dusted on a little tan eye shadow to make my blue eyes stand out. Then I put on my cutest jeans and a pink top with rhinestones on the snaps, and ran downstairs. I forced myself to swallow a bowl of cereal and drink some milk. By the time my dad was ready to drive me to school I was a nervous wreck.

"Don't you look pretty," he said, picking up a notebook stuffed with loose papers and cramming it into his briefcase. "What's the occasion?"

"I look that different?" Horrified, I looked into the new mirror in the entryway. I looked like I was ready to go to a party. "I was going to ask someone to go to a dance today, but if he thinks I got all fixed up—"

"You look great every day," my dad said. "Let's go."

"Let's see," my mom said, walking over to join us. "Whoa, wait a minute, Skylar. Not so fast," she said, looking at my shirt.

"What's wrong?" I asked, my stomach plunging. Not another argument about my clothes, since my mom is totally fashion-clueless.

"Your top is unbuttoned pretty far down. Don't you think?" she asked my dad. He shrugged.

"They're snaps, and they're not—"

She interrupted me. "And too many of them are unsnapped. You don't want to look cheap."

"It's not like you can see my bra or anything. I don't think I look cheap, do you?" I asked my dad, rounding my shoulders and trying to look as un-cheap as possible. My mom's foot was about to start tapping any second, I could tell.

"I'm going to stay out of this one," he said, laughing. "I'm not the fashion police."

"Oh fine, make me the bad guy," my mom said, reaching forward to snap me up.

"I can do it myself. I'm not five," I said, snapping my top all the way up to my neck. "Now do I look prissy enough for school?"

My mom looked hurt and her cheeks turned magenta. Now I'd done it. "Watch it, Skylar. You're one step away from getting grounded."

"Apologize to your mother," my dad said.

"I'm sorry," I said. "Can we please leave now?" I tugged open two snaps, and thought I might undo a third as soon as I got to school.

I didn't have the nerve to talk to Dustin during English. Emelyn stared at him through the whole class and Mrs. Mintin never stopped lecturing, so I decided to wait until Science to ask him.

By the time I got to Mr. Bidden's class I was so nervous that my heart was pounding. Worse yet, he had rearranged the desks again and now they formed a big circle. A lab table with a Bunsen burner on it sat in the middle. I was early and chose a desk with several empties on both sides. Dustin walked in right before the bell rang. After looking around the circle, he spotted me. My heart flipped over when he started to walk toward my desk.

I couldn't believe it. He grabbed the seat next to mine, just like he did on the first day of school. *Could Dustin Coles actually like me?*

The teacher set a rack of test tubes and an empty pan next to the Bunsen burner and turned it on. "What's he doing?" Dustin whispered.

"Making soup," I whispered back, and Dustin actually laughed out loud.

Mr. Bidden stared at us with a mean look on his mole-covered face. I looked down and pretended to take notes. What I really wrote was this:

Want to go to the backwards dance with me?

As soon as the teacher bent down to light the burner, I tore off the square of paper, folded it, and handed it to Dustin. I tried not to pee my pants while he opened it. Mr. Bidden heard the paper rustle and looked right at us. I panicked for a minute, worried that he would snatch the note and read it out loud to the whole class. But he just gave us another stern look and started to explain the experiment.

To my horror, Dustin just folded up the paper and

put it in his pocket. I couldn't even concentrate on the experiment. All I could think about was the fact that I'd just asked Dustin to go to the dance and he hadn't given me an answer. Was he saving my note while he collected other girls' invitations so he could pick the best one of us at the end? How long would I have to wait to get his answer? What if he never gave me one at all? Would I have to go through this nervousness a second time and ask him again?

Mr. Bidden warned us to pay attention, then poured some yellow fluid out of a test tube and into the pan that heated over the Bunsen burner. My stomach clenched. I'd seen my dad pour things from one test tube to another lots of times. That's how he'd speckled his forehead when I was six. I braced myself. And tapped on Dustin's desk.

"Watch this," I whispered. Dustin glanced at me and nodded. A blue flame shot out of the pan toward the ceiling, and some of the other kids jumped. So did I, even though I knew it was coming. I hoped Dustin hadn't noticed that I'd flinched.

"That was cool," he said, smiling at me as a puff of smoke evaporated.

Excellent!

"Your homework assignment tonight is to answer the questions at the end of chapter three and explain the chemical reaction you saw here today," Mr. Bidden told us.

We all wrote the assignment down in our notebooks. There was one minute of class left. Dustin touched the pocket containing my note and glanced over at me.

Here it comes! I thought. *He's going to tell me he'll go to the—*

The bell rang and Dustin stood up. "See you around," he said, and walked out of the classroom. I sat stunned in my seat with my invitation unanswered.

21
"He's off the scale!"

At the break, we went to the bathroom and Alexa brought up Smack's latest threat. "Skylar, this is serious. You *have* to tell your mom and dad they planted a dead rat in your drawer."

"Lex. No *way* am I telling them." I brushed my hair and put on lip gloss.

"Don't you know what that rat meant?" Alexa was more freaked out than I was. Now I was just mad. Crew Gang and their stupid threats were not intimidating me. Not even.

"It means they're out of ideas. It means they're trying to scare a thirteen-year-old girl because they're afraid I'll find Xandra's jewels before they will. They know I'm a better detective and they're quaking." I didn't want to admit that they were scaring me.

"Haven't you ever seen a mafia movie?" Alexa asked, looking at me dead serious. She leaned forward half an inch, staring at me like, *duh*. "That rat was a *message*, Skylar. You *have* to tell your parents that these creeps are threatening you."

Oh, sure. Then my mom would panic and call the cops. Forget about following Xandra's clues. My whole investigation would be ruined. "Alexa. This was a dead rat, not a picture of me with my head missing." I swallowed, trying not to touch my throat. "If I want to find Xandra's jewels, I can't say a word. To anyone."

* * *

My mom picked me up at the bottom of the hill after school. I'd re-snapped my third snap at the ten o'clock break when Alexa asked me if I knew it had come undone. "Why the long face?" my mom asked as soon as I got in the car.

Obviously I couldn't tell her everything that was bothering me. "I asked Dustin Coles to go to the backwards dance and he didn't give me an answer."

And I wasn't about to admit that I was afraid. If Crew Gang was threatening me with a dead rat and had possibly booby-trapped the dumbwaiter, what would they try next? I flicked the corner of my notebook over and over with my thumb. Then I stared at my mom, waiting for a reaction. She didn't say anything. "I'm sorry I was rude this morning," I mumbled. I'd said I was sorry before, but I didn't mean it so it didn't count.

"Apology accepted," she said, easing out into traffic. "Maybe Dustin's making you wait for his answer so you'll think he's a challenge," she said. Not a bad theory. My mom steered up the curving, woodsy streets that led to our house.

"But all the girls like him, Mom. He *is* a challenge. I'm sure I'm not the only one who asked him." I chewed my lip and looked out the window. "There's a lot of girls in our school who like him that are prettier than me, too." I pictured Emelyn Peters with her tan and her turned-up nose, flipping her hair around and giggling. Her mom let her get hundred-dollar jeans, and her chest was a lot bigger than mine, too. *Wasn't everybody's?*

"Not only are you beautiful and smart, but you're probably the most interesting girl who asked him," my mom said. "And if he has any brains he'll realize that, and he'll go to the dance with you. If he doesn't have brains, he would bore you to death anyway."

"Oh, he's got brains," I assured her. Picturing Emelyn Peters slow dancing with Dustin, I prayed that he'd say *yes*, and soon.

Before bed, I dusted my bathroom drawers for fingerprints. They were clean. No evidence. Then I washed and Windexed everything until the drawers and all of my makeup were spotless. I thought about leaving a snippy note for Smack to find, but decided against it. No need to let them know I was onto them. Better if they thought I was one step behind.

The next morning I skipped the eye shadow but squirted on some Ocean Fresh body spray. I put on another cute outfit, but I left out the sparkling barrettes.

Alexa wasn't at our locker so I walked down the hall by myself, ducking into the bathroom to freshen up my lip gloss before class started. After Alexa rushed through the classroom door and got into her seat I turned around and whispered, "This is driving me crazy. If he doesn't answer today I'm taking back my invitation."

"Don't worry," she whispered back. "He'll say *yes*. He's not answering right away so it doesn't look like he thinks it's a big deal who he goes with."

I looked at Alexa, wondering how she figured out stuff like that so fast. "He better give me some kind of answer," I said, wiggling my foot. "Even 'no' would be better than nothing."

"I bet you'll find out by tomorrow," she said, crossing her fingers.

"I wonder who else asked him." Taking out my compact, I angled the mirror so I could see over my shoulder, and spied on Emelyn Peters. A chubby girl named Sharon Greenburg had grabbed the seat next to her, probably hoping Emelyn's popularity would rub off. Sharon idolized Emelyn and tried to copy her, tossing frizzy brown hair over her shoulder and looking around with her nose in the air. Her nose wasn't cute or pointy, and she wasn't thin and tan, so the hair tossing had no effect on anyone.

Dustin's seat was at the end of the back row. He walked in right as the bell rang and I saw him smile at Emelyn as he squeezed past her desk.

"Hi *Dustin*," she said, looking up at him and blinking slowly. White-blonde hair flipped over a shoulder.

"Hi *Dustin*." Sharon copied Emelyn, looking up at Dustin through her thick glasses, trying to flirt. Unsuccessful.

I looked over at Alexa. "Dustin just smiled at Emelyn."

"You've got competition," she whispered back.

I faced the front of the class with my cheeks burning. *No wonder Dustin hadn't given me an answer yet. Maybe he really was waiting to see who else would ask him to the dance before he decided.* "If he doesn't tell me soon I'm going to ask someone else," I mumbled, knowing I would be crushed if he turned me down. There wasn't any other boy in our grade that I wanted to spend five minutes with, let alone slow-dance with.

"You need to be patient, Sky. He's cute, smart, and popular. Even if nobody else has asked him, there's no way he'd answer right away," she said quietly. For some reason

Alexa understood boys much better than I did. Maybe because she grew up with a big brother and watched how Ronnie acted around girls.

After class Alexa and I headed for the bathroom. A bunch of ninth-graders came in behind us, giggling and pushing past each other to get closer to the mirror. Alexa and I hung back, brushing our hair. We were just about to walk out of the bathroom when Emelyn Peters flung the door open and walked in with two of her friends. Alexa grabbed me and we backed into a stall together, closing the door just as one of them started to talk. I recognized Emelyn's harsh voice. "Oh *great*." She cussed loudly. "Does anyone have a tampon?"

"Here you go," someone said. A stall door slammed shut and I heard the sound of a wrapper crinkling. Figured she would have gotten her period before I did. Then she said something that lit my face on fire. "I'm gonna ask Dustin Coles to the backwards dance," Emelyn announced, and her girlfriends squealed. Alexa and I glared at each other, nose to nose in the little stall.

"He's off the scale!"

"Ten plus," one of them agreed.

"*Yeah* he is," Emelyn said loudly.

"When are you going to ask him?" somebody asked.

"I'm trying to get him to ditch class after lunch. See if he wants to go *shopping*. My brother's friend is a cashier at Gamers. He turns his back and blocks the security camera when I come in. Maybe I can get Dustin a little 'present.'"

"Something that will fit inside your jacket?" one of them suggested, and they all laughed.

136

"It's got big pockets," Emelyn said confidently.

Alexa and I stared at each other with our mouths open, listening to her friends giggle. Then we heard the bathroom door open and their voices echo away.

We hurried out of the bathroom and down the crowded hall, heading for our next class. "You could get her busted for shoplifting," Alexa whispered, triggering one of my private detective daydreams.

The French jewelry store was so exclusive that an armed guard stood in front of the door, watching each customer who walked inside. His nametag read, Bertrand. *A heavy black pistol weighed down the holster on his hip, and handcuffs dangled from his belt, ready for use. Bertrand's shoulders measured a yard across and his thighs were thick as tree trunks, yet he could run faster than the wind.*

He's no match for the international jewel thief I'm after, *I thought.*

Moments later, a tiny man disguised as a little old lady hobbled past Bertrand, who held the door open politely. My laser-vision glasses spotted the shotgun hidden in the suspect's cane, and before he could rob the store I had him tied up in a judo hold, begging for his release.

I shook off the fantasy as we rushed through the halls. Alexa had made me realize that reality was even more dangerous. "How? To bust Emelyn I'd have to cut class myself and follow them to the mall, then try to catch her in the act. I'm staying out of this one. It would probably blow up in my face. I'd get caught trying to bust her and then I'll be the school snitch. No way." I had enough challenges as it was.

"I guess you're right," Alexa agreed, "but you should

still tell somebody. See you at lunch." She smiled and waved. I raised my fingers, but couldn't manage to smile back.

We met at our locker at lunch, and Alexa jiggled her paper in front of my face. "I *killed* my math test. I only missed one."

"Awesome." I grabbed my sack lunch and we hurried through the halls and sat on the grass, pretending we didn't care where Dustin and Brendan were sitting.

Alexa unwrapped her sandwich and took a bite of baloney on wheat, then lowered her voice. "Have you seen Dustin?"

I looked around the lunch area and shook my head. The tables all around us were packed, but I didn't spot him. "I wonder if he went to Gamers with Emelyn so she could get him a new game. Without paying." I chewed a bite of my peanut butter and jelly sandwich. When I tried to swallow, it stuck in my throat like a wad of gum covered in dirt. I gulped some milk.

"They could be there right now." Alexa looked at me with big eyes, like I was missing a huge opportunity.

"What would you do?"

She thought for a minute. "I don't know. It's easy to say I'd rat on her. She's such a witch. But I don't like squealers either. It's a tough one. Well, you'll find out soon enough if he went with her."

"Next period," I agreed, so hoping he hadn't taken her up on the offer. Dustin wouldn't cut class so someone would steal something for him. *Would he?*

Alexa changed the subject and hunched forward

so no one around us could hear. "So did you figure out where the footprint map starts?" she asked, taking a sip of juice.

I shook my head. "I've been too busy with homework to try. But I can't wait to get back to it." I peeled the top off my blueberry yogurt carefully, trying not to fling pale purple goo onto my clothes.

"How about your secret agents?" Alexa asked, looking the tiniest bit jealous. "Have they helped?"

"Hunting Lion and Dragon Fire have posted some great ideas on my site. But unfortunately none of them have worked out so far."

Alexa looked a little bit relieved. So far no one had taken her place as my number one assistant agent. "Let me know what I can do." She took another bite of her sandwich.

"Want to come to my house after school? Maybe you can eat over. We can do the English homework together and then work on the mystery." She nodded, and I felt much better with my BFF ready to help. And knowing someone close by had my back, since Crew Gang was lurking around my house, searching for clues and making threats.

After I texted my mom and asked if Alexa could stay for dinner, she called her mother and got permission. Then she finished her sandwich and brushed crumbs off her lap. "So did you decide what to do about the dance?"

I set down my yogurt and looked around to see if anyone we knew could hear us. Some of Dustin's friends were sitting farther down at our table and the one behind us was full of jocks, so I bent forward and spoke softly.

"Maybe I'll ask him next period," I said, taking the last bite of my PB & J. "I might. If he comes to class."

Alexa stared at me with a little smile forming. "Come on, Skylar," she teased, "you may as well ask him again and I'll get my guts up and ask Brendan. Otherwise Emelyn might convince Dustin to go with her. We'll be nervous all weekend and by the time we work up our courage again they'll be going with someone else."

"You're right." The warning bell rang and we wadded up our trash. "Let's go."

There were three minutes left until the final bell rang and I had to be in Science. Dustin was nowhere to be seen. If he'd cut class to go to the mall with Emelyn to get a stolen game I wouldn't want to go to the dance with him anyway. Slipping through the doorway into the lab, I looked sideways down the hall. I scanned the faces of the last students who were hurrying to class, but I didn't see Emelyn or Dustin. I hurried across the room and took my seat at the last second. Would Dustin come to class? Or did he ditch with Emelyn?

Just as the bell rang Dustin rushed through the door, raced across the white tile floor and dove into the seat next to me. Mr. Bidden frowned at him and started his lecture. While I took notes I stole little glances at the pockets in Dustin's shirt and jeans. I didn't notice any suspicious, video-game-shaped bulges, and he wasn't carrying a backpack. I tried to work up the nerve to write him another note about the dance, but I couldn't figure out what to say. I also felt like I was begging him to go with me, and that really bugged me. So by the end of the class, I hadn't done anything about the dance at all.

I was really mad at myself for chickening out, too. But right when we stood up to leave, Dustin reached out and touched my arm. A tingle shot through my whole body.

"Hey," he said. I thought he looked a little nervous. And also very cute. "About the dance?"

My stomach plummeted. *He's going to tell me he's going to go with Emelyn.*

"Did you still want to go?" He looked at me with those big hazel eyes and my heart stopped.

"Um, yeah," I said stupidly, "if you do." I shifted my books into my other arm and we walked toward the door.

"Sure. See you later." Dustin smiled and headed away from me toward his next class.

Stepping out into the crowded hall, I was relieved that Emelyn and her friends were nowhere in sight. I leaned against the wall, pulled out my cell, and texted Alexa.

Dustin sd yes! :)

After last period I stood by our locker and absolutely could not wait for Alexa to get there so we could talk about Dustin. When she rounded the corner and headed toward me I bounced up and down and motioned for her to hurry.

Alexa rushed up to me. "What happened?"

"He asked me if I still wanted to go to the dance with him."

"What'd you say?"

"I was like," I made a silly face and crossed my eyes, "um, if you do." She laughed. "I'm such a dork." My stomach did an excited little lurch as I thought about it. Then I faced Alexa and smiled like I'd just won the lottery.

"Dustin is going to the dance with me!"

Alexa tossed her books into our locker. "I knew he would. I'm definitely asking Brendan tomorrow in English." She'd been putting it off too and crossed her fingers, looking at me hopefully.

"He's Dustin's BF. I'm sure he'll go with you." We started walking toward the bus stop. Dustin's brother skidded to a stop in a black Porsche, forcing a mom in a minivan to stomp on her brakes right in front of us. Dustin jogged down the sidewalk and hopped into his brother's car. I watched his tan fingers as they reached through the open window and closed the door.

Alexa elbowed me when she caught me staring, and I turned to face her. "So if Emelyn asked him to ditch class with her he must have turned her down. I don't know if she asked him to the dance yet…." My forehead wrinkled as I thought about it.

"But she isn't going to be very happy when he tells her he's going with you." Alexa laughed.

I thought about it for a minute, and didn't think it was funny. I knew there was going to be trouble.

22
Treasure Map

Alexa came over after school and I started my math homework while she tried to study for a history test. She kept fidgeting and changing positions on my bedroom floor, finally ending up cross-legged with the book propped open across her knees. Being dyslexic turns reading into a confusing nightmare. Alexa uses her index fingers to help her read. She puts her left finger under the word she's trying to sound out and covers up the rest of the sentence with her right, inching her fingers across the sentence a little at a time. The letters look jumbled and backward to her, and some of them seem interchangeable: *p* looks like *b*, and *q*, and *d*. I didn't understand how that was possible until she grabbed my sketchpad one day.

Alexa drew a quick cartoon of a pig's face and showed it to me. "What's this?"

"A pig."

She rotated the drawing onto its side. "Now what is it?"

"A pig," I repeated.

Alexa turned the sketchpad upside down. "How 'bout now?" I still didn't get it.

"Still a pig."

Alexa looked at me and nodded. "See? It still looks like a pig to you from every angle. Just like b *and* p *both look like* d *to me, just backwards or upside down," Alexa said, resting her chin in her hand and looking at the pig. "A d, b, p, or q is just a stick with a loop on one end of it no matter what direction the stick points."*

I looked at my BFF and felt so bad for her. "I can't imagine how hard that must be," was all I could think of to say.

I'd been waiting for the right moment to tell her I'd found something new that might help, and this was it. "Lex?" She looked up from the book with a grumpy expression on her face. "I've been reading about dyslexia online, and I think I have something new you could try."

"Anything." She closed the book, using her finger as a bookmark. "What?"

"A squishy ball, a clear blue plastic sheet, sunglasses, and vanilla-lavender incense."

"Huh?" Alexa wrinkled her nose, and then smiled when she realized I wasn't kidding.

"All those other 'cures' we've read about, the treatments that professors and doctors have come up with that haven't worked?" Alexa nodded. "Well I looked harder and I found an article that was written by an actual dyslexic." I smiled while I pulled things out of my bedside stand. "I know it sounds crazy, but try this." I handed her the squishy ball. "Put this in your left hand and knead it while you read. It's supposed to help you focus by keeping the other half of your brain occupied."

"I think I need both halves of my brain, at least," Alexa joked, "but I'll try anything. What are the sunglasses and the blue sheet for?"

"They're supposed to cut the light down to one color. Do you ever see colors when you're reading black writing on a white page?"

"Yes." Alexa looked shocked, like I'd just read her

mind. "I thought I was crazy, but I do."

"This article knows what it's talking about."

Alexa put the sunglasses on, covered her book with the blue plastic, and laughed. "I can't even see the letters now," she giggled. "Great cure for dyslexia."

"OK, Smartypants, take off the sunglasses." I lit the incense.

"Mmm. That smells good," Alexa said. "But why the incense?"

"When you get tested on the chapter, try to imagine the scent and it's supposed to help you remember what you read."

"OK," Alexa said, bending over her book and reading through the blue sheet while kneading the squishy ball with her left hand. I watched her for a minute and realized I'd been holding my breath. She wasn't squirming around anymore. I also realized Alexa wasn't reading out loud.

"Skylar, I think it's working. I don't know if I'll remember all this tomorrow, but I feel like I understand what I'm reading!" She crawled over to me and gave me a huge hug. "You're the best friend in the whole world."

"As soon as we finish English you can help me right back."

"You got it." Then her head whipped toward the doorway. Loud footsteps were clomping up the stairs. "Who's coming?" Alexa's face paled.

"Probably one of the guys in Crew—" Hard banging on my door interrupted me. My heart started to pound. Before I had a chance to stand up, the door flew open and Smack walked in with his legs wide apart and a smirk on his face.

"Sorry to innerupt," he said, casing my room. "But there's a short in the wiring somewhere and we gotta find it." He marched over to my closet and yanked the door open. "Mind if I look around?" he asked, already looking around.

"Help yourself." Alexa and I eyeballed each other.

I held up my index finger signing, 1, and finger-spelled, S-E-C. Then I bolted up the spiral staircase to my office, knowing Smack would demand to search it next.

A minute later the railing creaked as his heavy feet pounded up the stairs. I stood in the doorway to my office with my arms folded across my chest. "Find anything?" I asked with one eyebrow raised.

"Not yet," he snapped, glaring at me.

"Well look around," I said, gesturing around my little office while I backed up against the cupboard with the false ceiling. There was no way this guy would have an ultraviolet flashlight. Smack couldn't possibly imagine there might be a message written on the wall in invisible ink. But still. "Be my guest," I said nicely.

Smack nosed around my office, pretending to look for faulty wiring. He plugged a small device into the two electrical outlets and waited for the readings to register, nodding his head each time. "You're good," he grumbled before marching back down the stairs. He didn't know how good I was. I was so far ahead of those guys it wasn't even funny.

When I walked back into my bedroom Alexa and I stared at each other. "He gives me the creeps," she whispered.

146

ME TOO, I signed, making a *Y* with my hand and moving it back and forth between us. "Smack and his crew are always snooping around when they should be working," I whispered.

"Did you tell your parents?"

"No way. You know my mom panics when she thinks about me doing anything dangerous. And I have a feeling taking on these guys might qualify as dangerous."

"You think?" Alexa looked worried.

"Relax. I won't get into trouble. We're going to follow the clues and figure out where the jewels are hidden before they do. You with me?" Alexa hesitated before she slowly nodded.

She was right to be afraid.

We started our English homework and I read the chapter on verbs out loud while Alexa stared at me, listening carefully like she always did when we studied together. She kneaded the squishy ball, and when we got to the quiz at the end, she got almost every answer right. Now if she could just remember everything she'd learned when we got to class in the morning. "I can't study anymore," Alexa announced after an hour. "My brain's stuffed."

"That's OK, we're done with English and I can finish my essay later. Want to see the map now?"

My heart started to race and Alexa's cheeks turned pink. "Yes."

"Follow me." I led the way up the spiral staircase and we walked into my office. Pulling the metal box out of my desk, I unlocked it and took out the taped-together bird's nest clue.

"Wow," Alexa breathed, looking at the map. "Those

are the papers you found in the gazebo?"

"Uh-huh," I nodded, holding them carefully. "They're really fragile. Let's go downstairs and make a better copy." We ran down the two flights of stairs and went into my dad's gadget room.

"This looks just like a real laboratory," Alexa said, staring at one side of what used to be the ballroom. A long counter ran down that wall, covered with beakers and test tubes and burners and microscopes.

"That's because it is a real laboratory."

Alexa looked at me and made a face.

On the opposite side of the room, my dad's electric train set covered a big wooden table. When I flipped the switch, the train zipped through tunnels, in between potted plants, behind the aquarium, and past a clay model that he'd sculpted of his own head.

There was a big art piece on another wall that he made out of an old railroad sign and chunks of a train car he'd found at the junkyard. He welded it all together into a cool abstract that he called, "Train." When we first moved in he made a huge table out of scrap wood that sat in the middle of the room, covered with his "treasures." Sometimes my mom called it "his junk." This made both my dad and me mad. I loved his treasures and liked to collect my own. The first time she made the junk comment my dad told her she was too practical and needed to learn to think outside the box. He meant she should try to see things differently, and told her she should try new things: Explore. Be adventuresome! My mom tried a new recipe for dinner that night to prove that she could think outside the box.

"I love this room," Alexa said, looking around. "Your dad's so cool."

"Thanks." I smiled. "He really is. I've always loved his gadget room. I used to dig around in it in our old house when I was little and I'd always discover some hidden, unexpected thing. Like once I found a folded-up hundred-dollar bill in the caboose of his old train set. He'd just stuck it in there for fun and when I found it, he split it with me and let me put fifty dollars in my savings account. My grandpa and my dad both taught me to look everywhere for clues. I never know what I'll turn up if I search hard enough."

"I wish my dad was creative and knew how to teach me things like yours did," Alexa said wistfully. "Mine's such a—he's so boring." I knew she was trying hard not to call him a jerk.

"Maybe you need to teach him how to see things differently."

"Maybe I can someday," Alexa said hopefully, looking around the room.

Neat stuff that my dad dug up in the desert rested on shelves: fossils, ancient rocks, and an Indian arrowhead. He loved art, and the walls were covered with oil paintings, collages he'd put together, projects I'd made since kindergarten, and a scientific chart of the elements. Another wall was hidden by floor-to-ceiling bookshelves containing chemistry journals, over a hundred issues of *Scientific American*, construction manuals, and how-to books for do-it-yourselfers.

Across from the bookshelves there was a long desk topped with messy stacks of my dad's papers, a computer, and a printer. I turned on the printer and scanned the taped-together map. Moments later a grainy gray picture popped out. Alexa looked at it and frowned. I adjusted the brightness and contrast and hit *print* again. The machine spit out another page. The torn pieces of map had become one, and I had a good copy in my hand.

"Sweet," Alexa said.

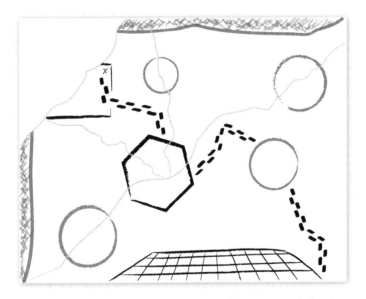

"Except there's a chunk missing," I answered, looking at the map.

Alexa bent over the photocopy. "We'll figure it out. Without the missing piece," she said confidently.

"*X* marks the spot," I said, pointing at it. "But where do we start to look for *X*?"

"Can I see?" Alexa picked up the map and stared at it. "Let's go back upstairs," she suggested.

We went back up to my office to work on the clue.

I spread the map out on my desk and stared at it with the annoying woodpecker tapping at my brain again. The footstep pattern, the circles in and around them, the hexagon, and the rectangle had a familiarity that bugged me. Knowing that I had the ability to figure it out and that the answer was hiding in my brain was driving me crazy. The map sat silently on my desk, teasing me. After staring at it some more, the disturbing feeling that this was a familiar pattern got worse.

"Can I look at it again?" Alexa picked up the map, staring at the paper and then stepping sideways around my little office as she looked out all of the narrow windows. I scanned the yard and gazed down into the canyon. The sun began to set, casting long shadows and an orangey glow across the mountains. Suddenly Alexa caught her breath. "Skylar—come here!"

"Girls? Dinner," my mom called.

My head whipped from one side of the room to the other. I looked at Alexa and then toward my door. We were completely out of time.

23
A Rusty Metal Box

J ust a second," I shouted, hurrying over to where
Alexa stood at the window.

"Look! Down there." She pointed toward the greenhouse, then at the rectangle on the map. "And there."
Alexa pointed to a tree near the gazebo, and then to one
of the circles on the map. I looked into the backyard. The
back of my neck prickled. Suddenly the circles, the hexagon, and the rectangle in between the footsteps made
sense. They stood for trees, the gazebo, and the greenhouse. Alexa had just figured out where to take footstep
number one.

My mom shouted for us again and I groaned, knowing we couldn't wait another second to go downstairs.

"It's OK," Alexa said. "We'll get right back to it after
we eat."

We gobbled down dinner as fast as we could, desperate to get into the backyard and follow the footstep
map before it got too dark. My parents kept interrupting
our fast chewing with questions. "So did Dustin give you
an answer about the dance?" My mom twirled spaghetti
around her fork.

"Mm-hm," I said, chewing a huge bite. "He's going."

My mom smiled. "He's pretty smart after all, isn't he?"

I rolled my eyes and took a swallow of milk. "I guess
he'd rather go to the dance with me than Emelyn." This
gave me a rush.

"Who's Emelyn?" my dad asked.

"This flirty blonde girl from Florida. She asked him to ditch fifth period and go to the mall so she could steal a game for him, but he turned her down." I chewed a mouthful of salad.

My mom set down her fork. "How do you know that?"

"He must have, because I have fifth period with him and that's when he said he'd go to the dance with me."

"I mean how do you know she asked him to go to a store and accept stolen merchandise?" She looked at me quietly while she waited for me to answer.

Uh-oh. I had just opened my big mouth a little too wide in front of my mom, the professor. Now I had to give her a complete answer or I'd get grilled on the details. The sun started to disappear behind the mountains. We didn't have much time.

"I overheard her in the bathroom. She told her friends she was going to ask Dustin to ditch his next class and go to Gamers, where the clerk is her brother's friend and would hide the security camera for her if she wanted to take something. Fifth period is Science, and he came to class, so he didn't go with her." I twirled spaghetti and waited for her next question. I knew what it would be.

"Did you report her?" my mom asked. Both of my parents had totally stopped eating and were staring at me. I heard Alexa swallowing milk.

"No." I had such a huge ball of pasta on the end of my fork there was no way I could get it in my mouth. I started untwirling.

"Why not?" my mom asked. My father took a bite of salad and looked at me thoughtfully while he chewed.

"*A*, I didn't know if she was really going to steal something or if she was just bragging to impress her friends. *B*, I had no evidence and I would have had to cut class to get proof. *C*, it's the first month of middle school and I don't want to be known as the school snitch."

There. That ought to do it.

My mom stared at me until I squirmed. "Those are not legitimate reasons, Skylar, and you know it. If one of your classmates is admitting to shoplifting and encouraging others to join her, it is your duty to report her."

"Samantha," my dad looked at my mom with a concerned expression on his face. "Let's not force Skylar to be a tattletale when she's not even sure whether this girl stole anything or not." I stopped eating. Suddenly I wasn't hungry anymore. I knew what was coming.

"She tried to get another student to cut class. We know that for a fact." My mom set her fork down carefully and looked at my dad. "Tattling is a non-issue." Whatever that meant. "Haven't we always taught Skylar not to compromise her ethics, no matter what anyone thinks?"

"Yes we have. And we've also taught her not to leap to conclusions, jump the gun, or snitch on her friends, especially if there's some doubt as to what they've really done," he answered calmly.

"Emelyn's not my friend," I mumbled.

My mom's lips disappeared and her eyebrows tightened. She hated it when my dad argued with her, especially in front of other people.

Alexa kicked me under the table. "Are you almost done?" I knew she felt uncomfortable listening to my parents fighting. Sometimes they acted like I wasn't even there.

"Yeah. Can we please be excused?"

"Sure. But clear your plates first," my dad said.

My mom just sat there looking at him while we scraped our chairs back and picked up our dishes. "I'll drive Alexa home now."

"It's too dark out to search the yard anyway," Alexa said as we ran up to my room to get her stuff. "You'll have to follow the map without me." She grabbed her backpack and slung it over her shoulder. Then she looked at me and her face softened. "You can do it, Skylar."

An hour later I was propped up in bed trying to write my essay. My parents' bedroom was right below mine and I could hear them arguing. My mom told my dad she wished he wouldn't disagree with her in front of me. He made a comment I couldn't hear. I turned down the volume on my iPod and took the Soundtrap out of my detective kit. After putting in the earbuds, I held the microphone an eighth of an inch from the floor. Their voices sounded fuzzy, but I could still make out what they were saying.

"Kids that age are going to cut class, lie, cheat, and steal things whether Skylar tattles on them or not," my dad said calmly. "You're asking her to butt her nose in where it doesn't belong. As long as Skylar's not doing it, don't make her be the bad guy at school. She'll end up making enemies and the other kids will continue to do what they want anyway."

I held my breath waiting for my mom's reply. Would she push my dad and force me to tell on Emelyn? That's all I needed. I could see the caption under my picture in the yearbook: "Skylar Robbins: Ugly-Sweater-Wearing Pacific School Snitch."

"I guess you're right," she finally answered. Then they started talking so quietly I couldn't hear them anymore. Turning off my Soundtrap, I stood up and took a deep breath, relieved that their fight seemed to be over. Wondering why my mom and dad didn't seem to argue unless it involved me, I finished my essay feeling small and guilty.

Then I hid under my covers and called Alexa. She didn't answer her cell so I texted her: **My parents just got in another fight about me. It sucks. But my dad talked my mom out of forcing me to snitch. So that's good, I guess. I'm sick of worrying about stupid Emelyn Peters. I'll search the yard before school and see where the map leads. Thanks for figuring out where it starts.**

I didn't know how I'd be able to sleep. The treasure map hidden inside my bedside stand was pecking at my brain.

The second my alarm went off I rolled out of bed, tossed my nightgown on the floor, and scrambled into sweats and my pink sneakers. Grabbing my Porta-detective kit, I crept downstairs. Relieved to find the kitchen and dining room empty, I sneaked into the backyard undetected. It didn't look anything like the map, so I tried to imagine the view from my office.

"That tree there is this circle," I mumbled, "and the hexagon on the map must be the gazebo, so I have to go over *there* to start." Even though the footsteps on the map seemed to lead toward the greenhouse, I figured I better follow them in order in case there were extra clues hidden along the way. I walked toward the side of the house opposite the canyon and backed up against the wall where the footsteps looked like they began.

Taking four steps, I curved to my left and took another three, then veered right for six. I hit the first tree marked on the map. I hunted around the base of the trunk and looked up carefully at every branch. No clues. I crossed behind the tree and went left five paces, then turned left for three and walked to the right four steps. The gazebo was right in front of me. *The hexagon.* I'd already searched the gazebo and found the partial map. Besides that it was clean. From the gazebo, I took three steps to my right, then walked forward six paces. I stopped at the doorway to the greenhouse, opened it, and stepped inside.

An array of empty clay pots and open cupboards faced me. Spider webs decorated with dead bugs hung in the corners. The greenhouse smelled like earthy soil and fertilizer. The sun rose over the ridge of the canyon, and shafts of light filtered through the tinted windows. A moth fluttered through the air and disappeared into a corner. My heart pounded in my chest. This felt right. Was I about to find Xandra's jewelry box?

After checking the map, I walked sideways three steps, but all I saw were stains on the floor and new plants on the counter next to me. I started picking up pots one at a time and peeking underneath them, hoping to see a big *X*, but I didn't find anything except stray bits of soil. I looked around in frustration. The greenhouse was really pretty empty.

Look for clues on the floor, all four walls, and the ceiling.

Getting down on my hands and knees, I took the mini-mag glass out of my Porta-detective kit and looked through it, searching the floor inch by inch. There was nothing on it but dirt. I looked at the map again. Three steps from the greenhouse door led to the *X*. A chunk of the map on the other side of the greenhouse was torn off. Had Smack found the missing piece?

I looked up at the ceiling, but just saw spider webs and mold. The cupboard next to me was empty and the drawer below it was gone. A gaping hole remained in its place. Kneeling on the ground, I bent over and peered through my magnifying glass. I examined one wooden strip of the floor at a time, looking for clues. When I got right up next to the cupboard, I brushed away the dirt that had collected near the edge. As I stared at it through my mag glass, my breath caught in my throat.

There was a tiny, faded *x* on one of the planks.

My heart started to pound. But what did the *x* mean? "Keep searching," I answered myself. "The empty cupboard in my office had a clue inside it," I reasoned, wishing I had my black light with me, "maybe there's a clue in this one." I stuck my head into the cupboard and looked all around, shining my penlight into the corners. Except for spider webs it was totally empty. *Was there a secret message on the wall, written in invisible ink?* I didn't dare go inside to get my ultraviolet light. My mom could figure out what I was up to. And besides, there wasn't time.

I stared at the faded *x*. It was written in black felt pen

and matched the *x* on the back of Xandra's picture: one line was squiggly and the other one was straight. *I bet she drew the* x *on the back of her picture so I would know I was headed in the right direction when I found this one.*

The morning sun started to heat up the greenhouse. The fertilizer stench was getting smellier. I ran my fingers around the edges of the old wooden plank and pressed on the corners. One of them wiggled! Xandra's old gardening tools were still hanging from hooks on the wall, and I grabbed a rusty weed digger. Planks in the floor had gaps in between them for drainage. I stuck the tool between two planks and pried up the one with the *x* on it. There was a shadowy foot of space between the wood floor and the dirt below it.

From far away, at the bottom of the hill, I heard an engine rumble.

Bending down close to the opening, I shined my light into the cavity. There was nothing right below the missing plank, but when I aimed the penlight at the side opposite the cupboard, something metallic winked back at me.

The sound of the engine grew a little louder.

Flattening my body onto the greenhouse floor, I reached my arm in as far as it would go. *My fingertips touched something.* Wiggling closer to the cupboard and stretching a little more, I felt something square and hard. I squeezed my body as close to the cupboard as possible, thrust my arm in until it felt like it was about to break off, and wrapped my fingers around the object hiding in the shadows. I pulled out a rusty metal box.

Had I just found Xandra Collins's jewels? I pressed

the plank back into place, stood up and whirled around, ready to run up to my office to find out what the box contained.

And I came face to face with my mom and dad.

"What's that, Skylar?" my dad asked.

My mouth went dry and my hands started to sweat. "Just a rusty metal box."

"We can see that," my mom said, reaching her hand forward. "What's in it?"

"I don't know. I was just about to go to up to my room and open it." I shifted my weight onto my other foot as she looked at me, waiting to see what I might be hiding as the engine noise became unmistakable.

"Why don't you open it right here?" my mom suggested, putting one hand on her hip. Smack's truck roared to a stop in front of our house and I heard doors open and slam.

"Uh, OK," I agreed. Like I had a choice. Balancing the box in one hand, I used the other one to pry open the lid. It came open with a squeak, and we all looked inside.

Inside the box there was a dead leaf with curvy edges, a metal buckle like you'd see on an airplane seatbelt, a dried flower, coiled twine, a packet of nasturtium seeds, and a broken measuring tape. "See, Mom, that's it." I held the open box for my parents to see, desperate to escape with it before Crew Gang clomped into the yard and caught me in the greenhouse holding Xandra's box of clues.

"Just some old junk," my dad said, squeezing my mom's shoulder. "Nothing to worry about."

"Breakfast is ready," she said, turning around and

heading for the door. I hurried after her, giddy with relief. She looked at me over her shoulder. "Don't you want to leave that dirty box here?"

"Uh," I stammered, "no—I'll clean it up. I want to plant the nasturtium seeds," I said, tucking the box under my arm.

They had no idea that this was the next batch of clues that would lead to the hidden jewels. And that Smack and Ignado were desperate to find them before I did.

I followed my parents out of the greenhouse right as Smack's crew walked through the gate into the side yard. Trying to hide Xandra's box under my hoodie, I looked up as they walked toward us. Ignado glared at me. Smack smirked like he had a big secret. The rest of the men gave me hard looks. Ignoring them, I skipped toward the house like the only thing on my mind was the strawberry Pop Tart I was about to eat for breakfast.

I had to figure out what these clues meant. *Fast.*

24
UN-invite

I was so anxious to work on the clues in the old metal box that I didn't know how I'd be able to make it through school. But as soon as I walked into English, I knew I had a big problem, and promptly forgot about the mystery.

Emelyn Peters was leaning against my desk, waiting for me. Sharon Greenburg and Pat Whitehead stood next to Emelyn with their arms folded across their chests. Pat was one of the tallest girls in school, and definitely the meanest next to Emelyn. All three of them had nasty looks on their faces and they stared at me as I walked down the aisle. What a day for Alexa to be late.

"Excuse me, Emelyn, but that's my desk." I shifted my notebook onto my other arm. She didn't move.

"So I've got something of yours, and you have something I want." She stared at me and her bloodshot blue eyes didn't blink.

"What?" I hoped they couldn't see how terrified I was.

"You know what I mean," she spat. "You were hiding in the bathroom stall yesterday. I saw you go in ahead of me, so don't try to deny it." She stood up and took a step toward me. "You heard me say I was going to ask Dustin Coles to go to the backwards dance and then you hurried up and asked him first." Emelyn was more muscular than I was and Pat Whitehead looked like a giant.

Was I about to get into my first fistfight?

"I'd already asked—"

"LIAR!" Emelyn shouted, knocking the notebook out of my arms. It landed on the floor with a splat, and all of the handouts from my classes spilled across the aisle. Sharon looked at me gleefully and kicked some of the papers farther away. Everyone stopped talking and turned to stare at us. The black and white clock made a jarring click in the silent classroom. There were four minutes left until the bell rang. The teacher was nowhere in sight.

"I *had* already asked him. Ask Dustin if you don't believe me." I bent down and picked up my notebook. My friend Jamal Jackson scooped up the messy pile of handouts that Sharon had kicked under his desk, straightened the papers out, and handed me the stack. He gave Sharon and Pat a hard look as I stuffed the pages into my notebook pocket.

Emelyn lowered her voice to a threatening whisper. "Well I'm going to go to the dance with him, so if you know what's good for you, you're going to UN-invite him. Today." She spun around and headed for her seat, just as Dustin and Brendan walked in. Emelyn didn't see them since her back was turned.

My cheeks were burning. I took a deep breath. "Or else what?" I asked politely. I pictured my grandfather folding his arms across his chest and nodding his head. He always encouraged me to stick up for myself and never back down from bullies. *Do what you know is right.* I especially loved one of his favorite sayings. It sounded like something soldiers would chant while they marched: *Don't take any guff from the riffraff.* I wished I had a whole army behind me while I waited for Emelyn's answer.

She didn't turn around. "Or you're going to get your butt kicked when you least expect it, that's what," she spat, spinning into her chair. My face felt like it was on fire. The whole class was silent, watching. Dustin looked at her with a weird expression on his face, halfway between amused and disgusted.

"Why don't you ask him who he wants to go with, since he just walked in and saw you make a fool of yourself," I said under my breath, and the girl who sat next to me nodded. Emelyn had just become an even more dangerous enemy.

Mrs. Mintin walked into the room and everyone got quiet. I felt sick all through English, wondering what would happen to me after class. When the bell rang, Emelyn waited in the doorway until I got to it and then elbowed me roughly when I walked through. She grabbed my arm and got right in my face. "*UN*-invite," she warned me. I smelled cigarettes on her bad breath. She stalked off toward her locker and I went the other way.

You're going to get your butt kicked. When you least expect it.

Well, I expected it any second, so I figured Emelyn would give me a couple of days to un-invite Dustin before she and Pat beat me up. So I had to act fast. Like right now. At the ten o'clock break, I told Alexa about the un-vitation while we hurried through the halls toward the cafeteria.

"That's pretty scary, Sky," she said, feeding coins into the vending machine. "Split?"

"Sure," I said, as a Snickers bar clunked into the tray

at the bottom. "It *is* scary."

Alexa ripped off the wrapper, bent the bar in two, and handed me half. "What are you going to do?"

"I have the beginning of a plan." I took the sticky piece but didn't take a bite. Suddenly I wasn't very hungry.

Alexa looked worried. "I hope you know what you're doing."

I was worried. "So do I."

Dustin ignored me when I got to Science, so I didn't even look at him or try to start a conversation. Mr. Bidden passed out quizzes and turned on an overhead projector. We were studying botany and had to identify as many plants as we could by the color and shape of their flowers and leaves. I stared at each slide, scribbling down my answers and waiting for class to end. Then I suffered through history, and finally the last bell rang and school was over. Time to put my plan into action.

I ran down the hall toward Emelyn's locker and hid around the corner while I waited for her to show up. She finally marched down the hall with Pat Whitehead at her side, and they walked toward the cafeteria, laughing loudly. The way their heads were bent together told me they were plotting something. That figured. I caught up to a crowd of kids several yards back and tried to hide myself behind the tallest guys. I spotted Alexa and put my finger against my lips as she hurried over. We took off, tailing Emelyn and Pat.

"What's up?" Alexa asked, trotting so she could keep up with me.

"I've seen Emelyn stealing snacks from the vending

machine almost every day after sixth period. Let's go!" I walked even faster, weaving in and out of slow groups of guys and giggling girls so we wouldn't lose them. "I'm sick of Emelyn bullying me, and it's time for me to stick up for myself."

Alexa looked at me sideways. "And what are you going to do, tell on her for ripping off a Butterfinger?"

"Not exactly. But it wouldn't hurt to have a picture of her doing it. Or better yet, a video."

"Caught in the act?" Alexa's freckled cheeks bunched up in a smile.

"Exactly." I pulled out my iPhone and touched the camera icon.

"There she goes," Alexa whispered, "Hurry!" We sped down the hall after Emelyn, heading for the cafeteria. Moments later her arm was way up inside the vending machine, grasping at a hanging sack of Cheetos. I aimed my phone and listened in satisfaction to the electronic kissing sound it made as it photographed Emelyn reaching for the bag.

A loser named Bart who spent most of his afternoons in detention walked up and joined them. Emelyn said something I couldn't hear, then Pat took one side of the machine and Bart took the other and they started rocking it back and forth. It made so much noise I was amazed that none of the hall monitors or teachers' assistants came out to see what was going on. I switched my iPhone to video mode, recording them while the vending machine quaked.

Bags fell off the hooks and into the bin at the bottom and Emelyn shouted, "Yeah!" She'd hit the snack jackpot.

After taking a quick look over her shoulder to see if anyone was coming, she scooped up packs of potato chips, Fritos, Cheetos, and sunflower seeds with a big grin on her face, then crammed the stolen snacks into her backpack. I knew she'd try to sell the ones she didn't eat.

"Yes," I whispered, looking at my phone and wondering what to do with the evidence.

Then a new message chirped and I felt my face heat up. "Oh no," I said, staring at the screen. Suddenly Emelyn's stolen potato chips didn't matter at all.

"What's wrong?" Alexa asked.

"Look." I showed her the text and her face went pale.

watch out snoop, don't be a rat

"Who wrote that?" Alexa whispered.

"The sender's blocked." I swallowed, looking at the threatening text. "But it has to be Crew Gang." We just stared at each other as I stuffed my phone back into my purse.

"How'd they even get your number?" Alexa's nose wrinkled.

"I told you, they're all over all of our stuff. My dad probably left his cell sitting around and they copied my number from his contacts."

"Pretty sneaky."

I smiled. "Not sneaky enough. I caught them."

She nodded. "Have you told your mom?"

"Of course not. You think I could admit that they're threatening me? She would force me to stop looking for Xandra's jewels, and you know there is no way—"

"Skylar." Alexa cut me off, raising one eyebrow. "Did you ever think that maybe your parents might be right once in a while? Maybe they know when you're getting in too deep and something bad could happen to you?" She looked at me like I was being stupid and careless. Like my mom warning me to be careful was a good idea when there was no *way* I was giving up on solving a case. It seemed like they were both shouting at me: *"Don't take unnecessary chances!"*

It made me mad, and I glared at my best friend for a second. Then I forced myself to calm down. "Thank you for caring about me. But nothing bad is going to happen. I'm smarter than they are, for one. And I'm way ahead of them. Those guys are a joke. The best they could come up with was putting a dead rat in my drawer? *Really?*"

Alexa took a deep breath and her cheeks turned pink. I knew she didn't want to spit out the words she was about to say. "You need to be more careful, Skylar."

I stared at my best friend, willing her to understand. "Pat Whitehead comes up with worse threats than those jokers. So please stop worrying, OK?"

Alexa just looked at me and shook her head.

If I were as smart as I thought I was, I would have listened to her.

25
The Thief in the Mirror

The next morning Alexa beat me to first period. I knew she had something to tell me as soon as I saw her pink cheeks, and I hurried into my seat. Alexa came up to my desk with an excited look on her face. She leaned over and whispered, "I just asked Brendan to the dance. He said *yes!*"

I smiled. "I knew he would. And he's friends with Dustin so hopefully they'll go together." My heart thudded as I pictured us double dating with the two cutest guys in school.

"Hopefully neither of them will cancel," Alexa said, crossing her fingers.

"I know, right?" I hadn't even thought of that. What if we got stood up on our first date, and had to walk into the backwards dance together like two losers?

"How about Emelyn and Pat robbing the vending machine? Did you show the video to anyone?"

"No. I can't decide what to do." I shoved my backpack under my chair, worrying about the evidence I had on my phone.

"Why don't you tell Dustin the truth, that Emelyn is threatening you if you don't un-invite him. Ask him what he thinks you should do. He's smart, and it does involve him."

"OK. Good idea." Emelyn walked in and we stopped talking. The bell rang and Alexa squeezed my arm before hurrying into her seat.

"Take out your textbooks, read chapter four, and answer the questions at the end," Mrs. Mintin told us. She hobbled over to her desk and began grading papers.

I opened my book and glanced at Alexa. She took the squishy ball out of her purse and squeezed it with her left hand. "Where's the blue sheet?" I whispered.

Alexa shot me a look. "I'm not bringing it to school," she hissed. "They make enough fun of me as it is. I'm not calling more attention to myself."

"OK. Think vanilla-lavender." She gave me a little nod. Her knees bounced up and down and her lips moved while she followed her finger across the page, trying to get through the chapter fast enough to answer the questions before class ended.

I finished the quiz quickly and had time to kill. Taking the compact out of my purse, I cupped the little circle of mirror in my palm, aimed it behind me and zeroed in on Emelyn. *That cheater was copying the answers right off Sharon Greenburg's paper!* Sharon's head was bent over her book and she didn't even notice. I continued to spy and couldn't believe what I saw next.

Emelyn looked sideways. When Sharon was distracted fishing through her purse, Emelyn swiped her favorite pen right off her desk. It was one of those expensive ones that came in a silver case. Last year Sharon made a big deal out of offering to let her friends use it when we were signing yearbooks. "Want to use my Cross pen?" she'd say, smiling proudly. Emelyn's purse sat open on the floor, and she dropped Sharon's silver pen right into it without even looking up from her quiz.

I scribbled a note, made sure Mrs. Mintin wasn't

looking, and tossed it to Alexa: *Emelyn just stole Sharon's Cross pen right off her desk!*

Alexa read the note slowly and then looked at me with her eyes wide and her mouth open. She started to look over her shoulder, but I shook my head and put my finger on my lips. "Wait," I mouthed.

She nodded, scribbling a note back to me: *And Elemyns suposed to be Sharens freinb!*

"Now!" I whispered to Alexa, jerking my head toward the back row. She turned around slowly pretending to crack her back, and peeked at Sharon and Emelyn. Looking into my mirror, I saw Emelyn sitting there with a smug grin on her face. Sharon looked like she was ready to cry.

Here's my chance to bust apart their little trio.

Class ended and Sharon stayed in her seat, rummaging through her purse and searching the area below her desk. I knew what she was looking for, and exactly where it was. Pat and Emelyn gave me dirty looks as they walked out, and they mouthed, "UN-invite," at me.

By the time science class started I had changed my mind ten times about what I was going to say to Dustin. No way was I going to un-invite him to the dance. Should I tell him Emelyn stole Sharon's pen? And that she told me I'd better un-invite him to the backwards dance, *or else*? Or would he think I made up a story about Emelyn stealing because she was threatening me? The dance was a week from Friday so I had to do something fast.

Dustin walked into class and I made a quick decision. I caught his eye and motioned for him to sit next to me. "What's up?" he asked, settling into his chair.

"Um, you've been on Student Council before, right?"
He nodded "Uh-huh."

"So can I ask your advice about something?"

"Sure." His big hazel eyes looked into mine and I almost forgot what I'd planned to say.

"OK, if you knew one of our classmates was stealing things, like out of other people's lockers, what would you do?"

"Boy or girl?"

"Huh?"

"The thief. Is it a boy or a girl?"

Oh-oh. It sure didn't take him long to figure out I was talking about a specific person. "Why does it matter?"

Dustin thought about it and grunted. "Huh. I guess it doesn't. So who's stealing?"

"I just wanted your opinion. You know, about snitching in general."

Dustin looked at me like he knew I was lying.

Great, I thought, *I'm asking for his advice about stealing and snitching and I'm lying while I'm doing it.* "Emelyn Peters," I blurted. "I saw her steal an expensive pen off someone's desk in English. I just wondered if I should say something." My heart raced while I watched his face, trying to figure out what he was thinking. Would he suspect this had something to do with the backwards dance? I knew Dustin had turned Emelyn down to go with me instead. Did he know I knew that Emelyn had asked him too? It was getting so confusing I felt like my head was about to explode.

"Whose pen?" Dustin asked.

Just like my mom, he had to have the details. "Sharon

Greenburg's."

"Why don't you just tell Sharon that Emelyn took her pen?" Dustin stared at me like, *how obvious was that?* He ran his fingers through his glossy hair and looked away.

Duh. Why hadn't I thought of it without asking him? And besides, did Sharon even deserve my help? I remembered the satisfied look on her face when she kicked my papers across the aisle. Dustin tapped his pencil on his desk like the whole issue was uninteresting.

"Good idea. Thanks," I said, opening my science book and dropping the subject like I was bored with it too. If he found out Emelyn was threatening to beat me up if I didn't un-invite him to the dance, he'd know I had a motive for ratting her out. Thanks to him, now it would be up to Sharon.

After class I walked down the hall by the cafeteria. I knew exactly where Sharon's locker was. She'd pasted stickers from a boy band all over it, then had gotten in trouble and was told to remove them. She tried, but strips of cute guys' heads still stuck to the door. I stood in front of her locker and waited. Moments later Sharon plodded down the hall, staring at her feet.

I stepped into her path. "Sharon," I whispered. She looked at me and backed up a smidge, like she was surprised that someone was actually talking to her. Curling my finger, I motioned for her to follow me around the corner like I had something Top Secret to tell her. Which I did. We hurried to the end of the hall and walked behind the wall, hiding in the teachers' parking lot. "I know who has your Cross pen."

Her mouth dropped open. "Who?"

"She's pretending to be your friend. You have to promise you won't say who told you."

Sharon nodded. "OK." She stared into my eyes, waiting to find out who had betrayed her. Afraid and angry at the same time. "Who stole it?"

"You need to tell a T.A. or a teacher. Don't just confront her or she'll deny it. Her purse needs to be searched. Today. By an adult. Understand?" I looked around. If one of them came out to the parking lot and caught us standing there we'd need an excuse, fast.

Sharon nodded. "Exactly. Who took it?"

"Emelyn Peters," I said quickly. "She stole it right off your desk in English."

Sharon's face fell as she realized the coolest girl in school wasn't so cool after all, and wasn't her friend either. Her eyebrows scrunched like what she decided to do would be life-changing. One of the biggest, most important choices she would ever make. Then she looked up at me and nodded, ever so slightly. Like a decision had been made.

"Come on. We have to get to class," I said, and we hurried back into the hall. Three cheerleaders marched toward us giggling loudly, then hushing their voices to a whisper when they passed as if their conversation was way too juicy to let us overhear.

Sharon watched them walk away, knowing they were in a club she would never be allowed to join. "I'm sorry I was mean to you in class," she said, staring at the ground. "Emelyn said you were trying to take Dustin away from her. And some other stuff about you that—probably isn't true." This made my stomach twitch. Sharon looked up at me through her glasses. "Nobody popular ever paid attention to me before."

"It's OK, Sharon," I said, forgiving her. "I get it."

"Yeah, right."

The look on her face told me I would never understand how she felt, and that she knew I really didn't get it at all. Didn't understand the loneliness she felt, because I had a BFF and other friends. Lots of Facebook likes popped up any time I posted anything, and I was in plenty of popular kids' Instagram pics. I didn't get the attention of every boy in our grade, but I got enough.

"OK," Sharon said, staring at her feet, then up at me. "So what should I do?"

I looked around to make sure none of Emelyn's friends were near enough to hear us. "You should tell somebody now, while she still has your pen on her. Otherwise it will be impossible to prove she stole it." I raked my hair behind my ear, hoping she would listen to me and take my advice. Hoping she wouldn't turn on me, run to Emelyn, and rat me out for snitching.

"You're right," Sharon said. She stomped down the hall, heading for Principal Martinez's office with a determination in her step that I'd never seen before. My stomach sank as I thought about what I'd started.

I didn't know it then, but my own nightmare was about to begin.

26
Punishment

fter school I had gymnastics practice and stretched, kicked, jumped, and tumbled until my muscles were aching and sweat was trickling down my sides. When I got home I was so slammed with homework that I didn't have time to worry about Emelyn Peters, UN-inviting Dustin, or Sharon Greenburg's stolen pen. I couldn't work on the clues in the rusty metal box with Smack's crew roaming all over our house, so I hid the box above the false ceiling in my office cupboard where I was pretty sure they wouldn't find it.

Taking a break from doing homework, I decided to go downstairs to watch TV. I headed down the first few stairs, and flinched when I saw Ignado coming up toward me with a mean look on his face. Seven steps separated us. I wasn't about to back off. So I climbed down two more steps.

Ignado stomped up three more stairs.

We stopped face to face and his brown eye glared at me. Ignado shook his head like he was giving me a warning. I moved to my right, and he waited a second before leaning sideways to let me pass. I skipped down the stairs with my heart beating hard, smelling the harsh stench of B.O. he had left behind.

Moments later I was in the den. I turned on the TV and flicked through the channels, but I didn't even notice what was on. Cartoons. A stupid show that was supposed to be funny. *What was Crew Gang up to?* Infomercial.

They have a clue that I don't have. Click, click, click. Sports. News. Danger. *Think.*

I pushed a button on the clicker, back to the news. "Tonight, clues left behind by an East L.A. gang led to their arrest in the recent desecration of several graves at the Forest Lawn cemetery." *Clues left behind.* Something I missed. The guilty smirk on Ignado's face.

Trigger.

Tearing up the spiral stairs to my office, I dragged the stepstool over to the cupboard. I reached up and removed the panel that hid the false ceiling, and then felt around with my hand. The rusty metal box was still there. Smack and his crew hadn't found it. I climbed off the stepstool and ran down the spiral staircase into my bedroom.

Peeking under my bed, I dragged out my detective kit. It was closed and locked, the digits still in the order I always leave them: 6-2-9. Crew Gang hadn't tampered with it.

But something was up. I sensed it.

I read a boring history chapter and studied for my science test. I kept my door open a crack so I could hear if anyone was coming. My parents insisted I keep an *A* average and I hadn't disappointed them yet, but elementary school had been easy. Middle school was a different story. Challenging in more ways than one, I thought, picturing Emelyn and her friends threatening me. Not to mention what was going on inside my very own house. **Dinner's ready**, my mom texted me just as I finished studying science, and I walked downstairs.

"Hi Skylar," my dad said, squeezing my shoulder. "How was school today?" We sat down at the table and my mom served up chicken, vegetables, and rice.

I pushed peas around on my plate, knowing I'd have trouble swallowing if I put a pile of them into my mouth. "OK," I lied. Then I set down my fork and my eyes filled with tears. I swiped them away with the back of my hand, hoping no one had noticed.

They had. My mom looked at me and forgot all about the food. "Honey, what's wrong?" She rested her hand on top of mine. My dad's jaw muscles bulged as he chewed a bite of chicken, watching my face while he waited for me to answer.

Gritting my teeth and forcing the tears away, I decided not to keep what was happening in school a secret any longer. The words tumbled out of my mouth so fast that they barely made sense. "Yesterday Emelyn Peters and her friends threatened to beat me up unless I un-invite Dustin to the dance, since she wants him to go with her. She said if I don't un-invite him I'll get my butt kicked when I least expect it."

"They threatened you?" my dad asked, looking at my mom and then at the phone like he was ready to stand up and do something about it.

And they're not the only ones, I thought, thinking about Crew Gang. "Then they gave me dirty looks all day, so I followed Emelyn after class—"

"You did?" My mom raised her eyebrows. Following someone to stand up for myself in a confrontation was so not me that she couldn't believe it.

When I remembered the evidence I'd gathered, I smiled. "—and I took a picture of her with her hand way up inside the vending machine."

My dad looked up from cutting into his chicken. "Stealing?"

"Uh-huh. I got her on my cell taking a whole bunch of snacks without paying."

"Good girl," my mom said. "Did you turn her in?"

"Not exactly."

My dad waited calmly for me to continue but my mom frowned. "Why not?" she asked.

"Because I saw her steal an expensive pen this morning, and then I did tell someone. Dustin Coles was on Student Council so I told him. He suggested I tell Sharon Greenburg, who Emelyn stole the pen from, and let her handle it."

My dad looked at me. "Good advice," he said, scooping up a forkful of peas. I knew he was debating something he wasn't saying. Like I could have done more. Should have taken charge. I wasn't exactly feeling good about my detective skills.

"I think you should have handled it yourself to make sure someone in authority found out," my mom said. She had completely stopped eating.

"They will, Mom. Sharon went straight to the principal's office after I told her who stole her Cross pen." I twisted the corner of my napkin into a tight spiral.

"Good for *her*," my mom said pointedly, like it should have been me marching down the hall and tattling instead.

"It's not like I just chickened out and haven't done anything," I said, sticking up for myself, "just because I didn't squeal on Emelyn myself." I took a small bite of rice.

"So Skylar," my father said, staring at me with a little smile on his face, "what else is there that you'd like to discuss with us?" He drummed his fingers on the table. My dad always saw right through me. I couldn't lie to him.

I set down my fork and took a deep breath. "I've been figuring out Xandra Collins's clues."

My mom and dad looked at me expectantly. It was time to come clean. So I spilled it.

By the time we were finished with our meal my parents were totally amazed with me. And unbelievably, they weren't mad. Yet.

I ran up the stairs ahead of them, eager to show them my detective notes and the box of clues. They had seen me tiptoeing around the backyard with the map in my hands, so they knew I was up to something. It felt so good not to have to sneak around behind their backs anymore that I could hardly stand it. The only thing I left out was the part about the construction workers threatening me. There was no way I could let my mom know I was searching for the jewels and getting terrorized by a bunch of bikers in the process. I'd be grounded for the rest of my life for taking risks again. No backwards dance, no jewels, no Dustin. No fun again, ever.

Forget it.

Besides, these jokers were so far behind me it wasn't even funny. I could post a YouTube video on how to locate clues and Smack couldn't find one if it was hidden in his underwear. They weren't scaring me off with their stupid threats. My mom and dad would definitely forbid me to continue my search if they knew I was putting myself in danger. But I knew I would find the jewels before Crew

Gang did.

They followed me up the spiral stairs and we crowded into my little office. I told them how the fingerprints in the dusty windowsill had led me to the cupboard. Then I shined my black light on the secret message so they could read it:

Congratulations. You found the first clue.

Here is the second clue: Things in this room are not always what they seem.

"After searching my office from top to bottom, I finally found an envelope hidden above a fake ceiling in the cupboard." I unlocked my clue box and showed them the symbol on the yellowed paper:

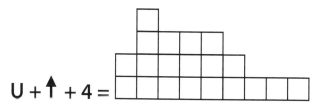

"I really had a hard time figuring out what the squares meant," I said. Then I stopped short, taking a deep breath. "OK. Now I have to admit something."

My dad folded his arms and my mom looked at me very seriously. "Yes, Skylar?" she asked.

Suddenly my tiny office was too small for the three of us. I needed some air but my mom was blocking the spiral staircase and I knew she wouldn't budge until I spit it out. "I knew the square design was the next clue to finding Xandra's hidden jewelry box, and I had already searched the whole house and the yard, so I knew it must be on a hidden floor. Remember Ms. Knight telling us there were either three or—"

My mom cut me off. "Yes," she said slowly. My dad waited with one eyebrow raised. I took a deep breath.

"Well, the clue says *you plus up plus four*, so I rode the dumbwaiter to get to the fourth floor."

"You did?" My dad shook his head and chuckled.

My mom glared at him, furious that he thought it was funny. Then she turned to me. "SKYLAR!" She shouted my name so hard that spit flew out of her mouth. "Do you realize how *dangerous* that was?"

Uh, yeah Mom, I did.

"It said the weight limit was 150 pounds, which is a lot more than me, so I figured it was safe." Looking down, I pretended to brush some dirt off one sneaker with my other foot, hoping this conversation would just go away.

My dad looked at me seriously. "Do you remember how old this house is?"

"One hundred years old," I recited.

"Correct," my mom snapped. "You risked your life riding in a metal box supported only by hundred-year-old cables."

"Nothing happened," I said meekly.

"And you didn't think you were taking a *risk*?" My mom scowled at me.

The metal wires holding the dumbwaiter up were old and might be rusty. They could snap in the middle of my ride, and I would plunge down three stories...

We could have a power failure and I could get trapped inside the wall.

I could starve to death or die of thirst.

While I was starving to death, the rats—

"I admit that I realized it was risky," I said, looking at the floor. I wasn't about to tell them I'd actually gotten stuck, and that if I hadn't found the emergency button I might still be trapped inside the dumbwaiter, banging on the walls and screaming.

"You got lucky. Next time you want to do something that you even suspect might be dangerous, you ask permission first, *understand*? You know better."

"I will, Mom. I'm sorry I didn't ask first. I knew I probably shouldn't ride the dumbwaiter, but I just had to find the hidden floor and the next clue. I promise I'll ask permission next time." I really did intend to.

"You bet you will. I am going to let you decide what your punishment should be."

"Honey." My dad touched my mom's arm, trying to calm her down. "I would have wanted to find the 'hidden floor' too." He made quotation marks in the air like he thought the hidden floor was just the attic, or maybe a storage area. I decided to let him believe just that, and keep the location of the secret floor to myself.

My mom wasn't going for it. She was *mad*. "And if you choose an easy punishment you will not be attending the backward dance." She stood there with her hands on her hips, waiting for my answer.

Oh no. I needed to think of something quick, and it had to be good.

I don't get an allowance. My parents made up a list of chores, and each one has a dollar amount next to it. For example, I got $3.00 for vacuuming our old house and $2.00 for dusting it, but when we moved into this big one I got a little raise. Still, I have to work hard on Saturdays to earn my spending money. Even though we have a cleaning woman, I still have to do chores. My parents think this will teach me "the value of a dollar," and "give me a good work ethic."

"How about two Saturdays doing chores without pay?" I suggested. This would totally stink, but anything was better than getting grounded with the dance coming up.

"Two full Saturdays, ten in the morning to three in the afternoon," my dad said.

"And next time you do something dangerous…." my mom warned. I could tell by the look in her eyes that I'd better think harder before I did something stupid again or I'd be grounded for sure.

"Well now that that's settled," my dad said, changing the subject, "what else did you find?" He loved hunting for treasures, just like me, and I think we were all relieved to get back to discussing the clues.

"I couldn't figure out what that weird drawing stood for, until I saw this pile of boxes. Inside one box was a picture of Xandra Collins." I pulled it out and showed it to them.

"She was beautiful," my mother said.

"Yeah she was. In the box below that there was a map with numbered footsteps on it. But some of the steps were missing. I found another part of the map lining the bird's nest in the gazebo. I must have remembered seeing paper in the nest from when we first looked at the house because I dreamt about it." I didn't tell them that there was a chunk missing, and that Smack probably had it. *Clues left behind.*

"You are quite the sleuth," my father said, and I smiled. "What happened next?"

"I put the map together and followed it to this hidden compartment in the greenhouse where I found the rusty metal box I showed you. The leaf, the buckle, the flower, the measuring tape, the seeds, and the twine are the next clues. I just have to figure out how they fit together. And remember what Ms. Knight said?"

"Which thing that she said?" my mom asked.

"That Xandra Collins had left a mysterious note saying whoever is smart enough and brave enough to follow the clues and figure out where she hid her jewels will inherit them? Well that smart, brave person is going to be me."

"Go for it," my dad said, and a moment later my mom nodded.

27
Busted

The next morning I walked into English feeling nervous, but confident. My parents' faith in me had given me courage. I ignored Emelyn's dirty look and sat down at my desk. Pat walked slowly down my row taking the long way to her seat, and when she passed me, she mouthed, "UN-invite," with an ugly sneer on her face. I ignored her too.

I should have paid attention to both of them.

Alexa scribbled me a note: **what hapenned with elemyn?**

I told Dustin that Emelyn took Sharon's pen and he said I should tell Sharon, so I did. I told her to tell a T.A. or a teacher. I'm sick of thinking about it and of my parents fighting about what I should do.

Im sick of elemyn caling me dislexa. I hope she gets what she desreves.

Class passed, and nothing happened to Emelyn. But lunch was a different story.

"I'm getting the chili," Alexa said, grabbing a bowl and a green salad as we moved through the cafeteria line.

"I'm having a sub. Tell me if I have anything stuck in my teeth when we're done, OK? I don't want to wear any salami to Science."

We headed toward an open table when all of a sudden Alexa stopped and grabbed my arm. "Look over there. *Cops.*" Two police officers walked across campus toward the principal's office. "Did you ever send anybody the pictures or the video?"

"No. Not yet." I didn't think stealing an armload of Cheetos would have brought the police to Pacific, but you never knew what else Emelyn Peters could have done.

We sat down at the very end of the table so we had a good view of what was going on. Emelyn sat on the lawn surrounded by Pat, Trish, and a handful of guys. Emelyn glanced over at the cops and didn't even flinch. Dustin was at a table near us, eating with his friends. The dark-haired boys at the far end of our table started speaking quietly in Spanish and pointing. One by one, heads turned as the word *cops* and *policía* spread across the lunch area. The police walked toward the principal's office and through the door to its reception area.

"Sharon must have told the principal Emelyn stole her pen," I said. "I hope she didn't say I was the one who told her." I tore a bite off my sub and chewed it like a dog gnawing on a sausage treat. Sometimes when I get nervous I feel like I'm starving.

"Do you think they're going to search Emelyn's purse?" Alexa asked me. "Or her locker?"

"Probably. Wait. Here they come."

The cops, the principal, and the vice principal came out of the offices and marched across the lawn toward us. I had the terrifying thought that they were going to walk right up to me and accuse me of taking sneaky videos while the whole school watched. But they stopped when they reached Emelyn and her friends. She stood up and started gesturing and shaking her head.

"I wonder if she has stolen games in her purse," I said.

"Or if she still has all those bags of snacks. They'll figure out she was the one who vandalized the vending machine."

"They broke it?"

Alexa nodded. "It has an *OUT OF ORDER* sign on it now." The cops walked back toward the principal's office, and Emelyn, the principal, and the vice principal followed. "Is she getting arrested?" Alexa squeaked.

"I don't think so. Not yet anyway."

Sharon hurried down the hall and followed them inside.

"Somebody's *busted*," a cute boy at Dustin's table said loudly.

"She's in truh-bull," Brendan sang.

"Emelyn is finally getting what she deserves," Alexa said. We looked at each other and nodded.

My satisfaction didn't last long.

The next morning, Emelyn didn't show up for English. Rumors were flying. Did Emelyn get arrested? Was she locked up in Juvenile Hall? Or did she just cut class again? Dustin came right up to me as soon as I walked into the room and asked me if I had heard what had happened. His blue flannel shirt looked so soft it distracted me. I looked away while I tried to figure out what to say. Then I looked back at him—right into his eyes. "I took your advice and told Sharon that Emelyn took her Cross pen, and I think she told the principal. Do you know why the cops were here?"

Dustin shook his head. "Uh-uh. But I think Emelyn got suspended. She's rude, anyway," he said, surprising me. "She really talked some trash about you." He took a step closer to me and I felt my face grow hot, wondering what she had told him. "Emelyn said you were going to un-invite me to the dance. That you changed your mind and didn't want me to go with you. She said you wanted to go with Brendan instead." He looked at me with those awesome hazel eyes and I felt my jaw drop open.

"Brendan Tadman? No way." As if I would ever betray Alexa and ask him. "She's lying. I was never going to un-invite you, even after she threatened to beat me up if I didn't." I looked Dustin right in the eye. I think he knew I was telling the truth.

He clenched his jaw and shook his head. "That's what she was talking about when she said you were going to get your butt kicked? How weak. She must be jealous." Dustin smiled at me, and then looked at the floor with an embarrassed expression on his face. *Did Dustin Coles actually just admit that he liked me? I know he said yes to the dance, but this made it sound like he* liked me *liked me!* He sat down, opened his book, and completely ignored me for the rest of the period.

I whipped out my notepad and made a quick note on something yummy to think about later: Dustin thinks Emelyn has a reason to be jealous of me! My heart didn't stop hammering for the rest of the day.

By sixth period, the news was all over campus. When the police searched Emelyn's purse they found Sharon Greenburg's Cross pen, plus a bonus: two stolen video games with the price tags and barcode stickers still on them, and enough bags of snacks to link her to the broken vending machine. Emelyn got suspended, but only for two days since it was her first offense at Pacific. She was following in her brother's footsteps. If she got in trouble again or was caught stealing she could get expelled. Best of all, she would not be allowed to participate in any after-school activities. Emelyn was barred from the backwards dance!

And I had a big secret. Skylar Robbins was the squealer who spied on Emelyn, saw her steal the Cross pen, and told Sharon. I had started the whole snitching process. But I hadn't officially told a teacher, just Dustin and Sharon. Did that count? Was I the official Pacific Middle School Snitch? Or just the snitcher's accomplice? I didn't want to be a tattletale, but I wasn't about to turn my back on a crime either. My brain was beginning to hurt from thinking about it.

28
The Setup

By Tuesday Emelyn Peters was back in school. English class started out normally. Mrs. Mintin got to her feet and held up the teacher's edition of the English book. "Please read the poem on page seventy. Then I would like you to write two paragraphs describing the symbolism the author used and how you interpret it." Alexa looked at me with a worried expression on her face. Expecting Alexa to write a good paragraph was like handing a blind person a paintbrush and waiting for a masterpiece.

"Use your imagination," I whispered. "Pretend the poem is a painting and just describe what you see." Alexa smiled gratefully and nodded. A few minutes later we were all concentrating so hard on describing the imagery in the poem that I never noticed what was going on behind my back.

Right before the bell rang, Mrs. Mintin collected our papers and gave us a homework assignment. Just as she finished explaining it, Jamal shouted, "Hey!" His eyes darted around the classroom.

Mrs. Mintin flinched. "Yes, Jamal?"

"My iPod's missing," he said angrily.

"You definitely had it when you came to class?" The teacher looked at each of us like if she stared hard enough the juvenile delinquent who took it would just give it up and raise his hand.

"Always keep it right here in this pocket," Jamal said,

patting his backpack. We all knew this was true, since he plugged in his earbuds and listened to rap and hip-hop between each class and on every break. "Had it when I got here. Now it's gone." Jamal gave everyone sitting near him a dark look.

For a minute, no one spoke. Then Emelyn said quietly, "I know where it is." She dropped her head into her hand, like ratting any of us out would absolutely destroy her.

Half the class whirled around to hear the thief's name. "Who took it?" Jamal demanded.

"Where is the iPod?" Mrs. Mintin asked Emelyn.

Emelyn looked down into her lap and hesitated. "I'm not a snitch," she mumbled.

Mrs. Mintin folded her arms across her bony chest. "No one is leaving this classroom until Jamal's iPod is returned."

The girls sitting near me fidgeted nervously. Emelyn looked around with a panicky expression on her face, like it was going to kill her to call out the thief. Grabbing her hair like an overacting starlet, she finally spat out the name. "OK, since you're forcing me to tell—I saw *Skylar Robbins* steal Jamal's iPod and put it in her backpack."

I felt like the air had been vacuumed out of my lungs.

"No way," Alexa said, her cheeks turning bright pink. The girl in front of her leaned away from me like I had something contagious.

"Oh right, Emelyn," I said. "Jamal's my *friend*." As if I would even steal anything from someone who wasn't my friend.

"Well, here's an easy solution," Mrs. Mintin said,

hobbling down the aisle toward my seat. "May I see your backpack please?" She reached a crooked hand in my direction.

"Of course," I said, handing it over.

Then I heard a snicker. Looked sideways. The smirk on Pat Whitehead's face sent a chill down my spine. Her pale eyes disappeared into slits. A vision of what was about to happen shot into my brain like I was looking into a crystal ball. The bell rang, but nobody moved. Mrs. Mintin reached into my backpack. A strange look transformed her face. Her hand came out in slow motion and my mouth fell open in disbelief.

"But I didn't—"

The teacher sighed and shook her head, holding up the iPod. "Jamal, is this yours?"

"That's mine all right." Jamal looked at me like I'd just farted on his birthday cake. "Thanks, Skylar. I guess I just figured out who my real friends are."

29
Porta-Detective Kit

Mrs. Mintin handed Jamal his iPod and gave me a stern look. "The rest of you may go to your next class. Except Skylar." She pointed a wrinkled finger at me. "You're headed for the principal's office."

My frozen brain finally kicked into gear. "Wait," I begged. "Jamal. Please, you have to believe me. I didn't steal your iPod." He rolled his eyes like my lie was too dumb for words. "I can prove it. But you have to give it back to me."

"Oh *right*." I watched in horror as he slid his iPod into his backpack pocket, possibly smearing the only evidence that could save me. His skinny legs propelled him out the door, leaving me alone with Mrs. Mintin while we waited for a T.A. to come walk me to the principal's office.

Five minutes later I was sitting on a couch in the reception area outside Principal Martinez's office, so mad I was shaking. Someone had stolen Jamal's iPod and planted it in my backpack. It didn't take a detective to read the smug look on Pat Whitehead's face and to figure out that Emelyn was behind it. She wanted to get me in trouble for more than one reason. If I got caught stealing she wouldn't be the only thief at Pacific. I could get suspended too, and I wouldn't be able to go to the dance with Dustin. I had to prove my innocence. But the evidence I needed was far out of my reach, and worse yet, it may have already been destroyed.

Mr. Martinez finally opened the door and motioned

me inside. I sat down in the chair in front of his desk, desperate to tell him my side of the story. The principal's brown suit was a little bit wrinkled, and his thick black hair shot up from his head like it was trying to escape. He pressed stubby fingers together and stared at me with one eyebrow raised like he'd already decided I was guilty. Mr. Martinez sat quietly for so long that I started to squirm in my seat, trying to work up the courage to defend myself. His office was so stuffy it was hard to breathe. Finally I couldn't stand the silence another second. "I didn't—"

"I think I need to call the police." Mr. Martinez slowly reached for the telephone, keeping his eyes on my face.

"Wait!" I pleaded. *If I got arrested and ended up with a criminal record, I couldn't become an undercover detective, could I?* Was my career about to be ruined before it even began? To my dismay, tears flooded my eyes, making me look even guiltier. The principal continued to tap the telephone keypad and stare at me. A little smirk twitched the corners of his mouth. I gritted my teeth and looked him right in the eye. "What's so funny?"

"Oh, this is just so typical." He leaned back in his chair and stretched, like he didn't have a care in the world. "Every student who is sent to my office swears they are innocent. And you can't all be innocent, can you?" He leaned forward and his black eyes bored into mine.

I stared right back at him. I didn't care about all the other students who got sent to his office. "I am innocent."

"That's what they all say."

"I didn't steal that iPod. Just give me a chance to prove it."

"I'd love to see that proof, Skylar." He smiled like he

195

thought he'd just beat me in some game we were playing.

"And I'll show it to you. Please call Jamal Jackson to your office, Mr. Martinez. Right away. Please."

Amazingly, the principal paged Jamal and got him out of class. While we waited for him to walk to the office I took my Porta-detective kit out of my backpack. If my hunch was right, it was about to save my skin. Unless Jamal had already smeared the real thief's prints beyond recognition.

I opened my Porta-detective kit and took out my Uni-printer. This was a one-inch square stamp pad with black ink and a tiny tablet of paper attached to the back. Just big enough to take one fingerprint. I set the Uniprinter on the principal's desk. "Mr. Martinez, I am now going to fingerprint myself with you as a witness."

I pressed my right index finger onto the stamp pad, then turned the Uniprinter over and rolled my inky fingertip across one of the small squares of paper. I tore it off and handed it to the principal. "See that? My fingerprint type is called a radial loop." Mr. Martinez squinted at the postage stamp-sized piece of paper I handed him.

"Want to look at it through my magnifying glass?"

He shook his head, but held onto my print. "I'll take your word for it."

Digging back into my Porta-detective kit, I pulled out a tiny packet of black fingerprinting powder and a little brush as Jamal walked through the door. "My fingerprints will not be on Jamal's iPod, because I did not steal it," I said confidently. "But I'm positive I know who did, and who set me up, and I'm about to prove it. Jamal, please set your iPod on the desk, and really try not to smear any prints that might be on it. *Please*."

After giving me a quick nod, Jamal carefully took his iPod out of his backpack, grasping just the edges with his fingertips. He set it down on the principal's desk and said, "Let's do this."

I sprinkled black dusting powder onto the iPod's shiny surface, spread it around with the brush, and whisked away the excess. The remaining black dust stuck to a whole gang of fingerprints. I looked at them through my Mini-mag glass. Most were a common spiral pattern called a whorl. But not all of them. There was a rare peacock's eye print right on the top of the iPad, clear and crisp.

"Jamal, let me see your fingertip." Holding his finger in one hand, I looked at it through the mag glass and nodded to myself. "Mm-hm. Your prints are the basic whorl pattern. And I'll bet Pat Whitehead's have a peacock's eye in the center. That's very rare. I have radial loop fingerprints, and there are no radial loops on this iPod." I lifted two well-defined peacock's eyes onto white fingerprinting tape and pasted the tape onto a Case Solution card. Then I turned the iPod over and dusted the other side. After peering at it through the glass, I offered the iPod and Mini-mag to Jamal. "Want to take a look? There are no radial loops on this side either." Jamal gave me a little smile and shook his head. I could tell he believed me.

One down, one to go.

I handed the Case Solution card to the principal. "If you will please call Pat Whitehead into your office and let me fingerprint her, I will prove she was the one who stole Jamal's iPod and planted it in my backpack. I guarantee her prints are peacock's eyes and will match the ones on that card."

Mr. Martinez raised his eyebrows and his cheeks reddened like he was watching an exciting TV show. Or like he was on Jeopardy and didn't know the answer to an easy question. "If I pull her out of class and you're bluffing, you're in for a long spell of detention," he said, glaring at me.

"I'm not bluffing," I assured him. "As soon I fingerprint her you'll know I'm telling the truth." The principal scribbled *Whitehead* on the card.

Jamal glanced at the clock. "Can I go back to class?"

"Don't you want to follow through and determine how your iPod wound up in this young lady's possession?"

Jamal looked at me and shook his head. "Nah, Sky's straight. She's tellin' the truth. Pat Whitehead and her crew have a hate on for Skylar for some reason. Besides, she wouldn'ta busted out all the fingerprint gear if she'd took it." He winked at me.

"Thanks, Jamal."

"No worries," he said, reaching for the door.

"You can go too, Skylar," Mr. Martinez told me. He

blew some stray black powder off the edge of his desk. "I do plan to have a discussion with Pat Whitehead about this, and I will also note the incident in her file. But I don't see the need to pull her out of class or do any more fingerprinting."

"That's fine with me. Sorry about the mess."

"It's all right." The principal looked up at me as if he knew I'd won the game, and was OK with it. "It was interesting," he admitted.

I packed up my Porta-detective kit and stood there fidgeting for a minute. "Why don't we just forget the whole thing?" If Pat and Emelyn knew I'd squealed on them to the principal they'd try to get revenge for sure. Dropping The Case of the Stolen iPod sounded like a really good idea.

Mr. Martinez drummed his fingertips on his desk and stared at me. "All right, Skylar," he finally said. "Since Jamal didn't want to take this any further, I'm willing to let the matter drop. Go ahead and get to class. I sincerely hope I won't see you in my office again. Keep your nose clean."

As if it had ever been dirty. "It is clean, and I just proved it," I said, pointing at the Uniprint he held in his hand.

He glanced at my fingerprint, tapped his desk, and then looked at me. "My apologies, Skylar. That you did."

30
The Final Clue

After school, I had to do something to get my mind off Emelyn and Pat, so I decided to work on the clues I found under the greenhouse floor. A leaf, a buckle, a dead flower, a measuring tape, a packet of seeds, and some twine. What did they mean? Once again, Xandra had me stumped. I felt like I knew how her mind worked after following so many of her clues, but this one was a real puzzle.

Leaf, buckle, flower, measuring tape, seeds, twine.

Some of those were things you could wear: a twine belt with a buckle, a flower in your hair. But what did that tell me about where Xandra had hidden her jewelry box? Did the kidnappers have it? Did she have it on her? Where was Xandra anyway?

I walked past Smack into the backyard and felt his eyes drilling holes in my back the whole way. Whatever. He didn't know what I was doing and he wouldn't be able to follow the clues I'd found if he watched me and took notes. If they thought putting poop on my makeup and sticking a dead rat in my drawer like a bunch of third graders was going to slow me down they were wrong. They were just trying to scare me, and it wasn't working. Not enough to stop me, anyway.

I sat down on the bench in the gazebo and stared into the rusty box. The buckle was made of metal. It was hard and sturdy. The twine was braided with four thin strands of golden fiber. Long and strong. The aged flower and leaf were unlike the buckle and twine. They were frail. Fragile. Dead. Decomposing. Turning to dust. The exact opposite of the nasturtium seeds: life, promise, growth, beginnings.

I unrolled the measuring tape. It was made of cloth covered with cracked yellow plastic and had numbers and lines printed on it. The end of it was missing. Someone had cut off the tape at five feet, eight inches. What did it all mean? Was that Xandra's height?

I picked up the packet of nasturtium seeds and turned it over in my hands. The edges were stained light brown and were starting to peel apart. I looked at the red, orange, and yellow flowers pictured on the package. "Why would anyone need nasturtium seeds in Santa Monica when they grow wild all over the place?" I asked myself. "Unless—nasturtiums are a *clue*." I looked back toward the house. Smack was standing in the doorway, staring at me. I waved and smiled, showing all of my teeth. Like I was just a dumb kid, playing. He turned around and went inside.

I gently peeled open the top of the envelope. The glue had completely dried out and the packet opened easily. When I peeked inside, my knees jiggled up and down with excitement. There was a message written on the inside of the seed packet in a spidery black scrawl. It looked like it was written with the same fine-point felt pen that drew the footstep map. "Office!" I said to myself, rushing out of the gazebo and running across the yard.

This could be the final clue! I thought, racing past Smack and bounding up the stairs to my room. Grabbing the banister, I pulled myself up the spiral staircase to my office and spun into my desk chair. Opening the rusty metal box, I tipped the lid back so I would have a container to pour the seeds into. I tilted the packet and the tan seeds bounced over each other as they rolled into the lid like dried-out raisins. Then something tinkled as metal hit metal.

I sucked in my breath and picked up a tiny gold key. I knew what it would unlock. If only I could find it. Turning my attention back to the empty seed packet, I ran my letter-opener gently between the seams until I had them all peeled apart. I spread the packet flat on my desk and read the message that was written inside.

Congratulations. If you are the smart, brave soul who followed clues to locate this box rather than stumbling on it by accident, you know exactly what this key unlocks. Your final challenge is to put these last clues together in the proper order, pinpoint the exact location, then use the key. At the end of the rope you will find the beginning of new adventure. Good luck.

And it was signed, Xandra Collins.

By the time I finished reading Xandra's note my heart was racing. "It *is* the key to her jewelry box," I breathed, staring into the confusing collection of clues. *If only I can figure out where she hid it.* I ran my fingers over the buckle, the twine, and the measuring tape, then dropped the seeds into an envelope and put it in my desk. Opening the secret compartment behind the middle drawer, I hid the golden key. My office was stuffy. I needed some fresh air to clear my head.

Running back down to my bedroom I looked at the clock. *5 p.m.* Quitting time. Two seconds later I heard Smack's truck start and rumble down our hill.

Excellent.

I hurried down the stairs and ran outside. Carried the box into the backyard and set the contents on the grass. First I uncoiled the twine and tugged it into a straight line. Then I measured it using the broken tape. The twine was twelve-and-a-half feet long. Jogging over to the guardrail, I stood at the very beginning of it and looked down its length as it curved around our yard. Then I bent over the railing and stared down into the canyon, the black metal cool underneath my fingers. Yellow-flowering mustard weeds sprouted in between jagged boulders. Nasturtiums grew in puffy clumps. Their bright yellow, red, and orange blossoms peeked out from between round leaves that looked like pale green lily pads.

The mustard plants had broad green leaves with curvy edges. I remembered learning how to identify plants during botany in Mr. Bidden's class. Suddenly I caught my breath and looked back into the box of clues. The crumbling brown leaf had the same shape as the leaves on the mustard weeds. The dead flower had tiny shriveled petals attached to its withered stem. They grew in clusters, just like mustard flowers. I picked it up and sniffed the petals to see if I smelled mustard, but they just smelled like dust.

Pulling the twine up off the grass, I held onto one end and tossed the rest of it over the railing. The end of it dangled near some mustard weeds. "But which one is the right plant?" I said aloud, running next to the railing and looking over. There must have been hundreds of batches of weeds and flowers growing next to and around each other. "How far down the guardrail do I—"

I stopped in my tracks and raced back to the part of

the yard where I'd left the measuring tape and snatched it up. "Five feet, eight inches," I said breathlessly. Starting at the far end of the guardrail, I measured off five feet, eight inches. I held one end of the twine and tossed the other end over the edge. The end stopped at a boulder that jutted out of the mountainside. No mustard weeds. No flowers.

"That's not it."

Running down to the other end of the guardrail, I measured five feet, eight inches down the rail and threw the end of the twine over the railing. The end dangled twelve-and-a-half feet down the canyon side and landed right at a thick batch of mustard plants. They were entwined with flowering nasturtium vines. Was Xandra's jewelry box just twelve-and-a-half feet out of my reach?

Hanging over the railing, I imagined trying to climb down the hillside without plunging into the canyon and breaking my neck. There was no way I could do it by myself. If my mom thought riding the dumbwaiter was dangerous she would completely lose it if I tried this. And I had no time to waste. I had to try to find the jewels before Smack and his boys came back or my parents got home from work. Yanking the phone out of my pocket, I speed-dialed Alexa.

"Hey Skylar, what's—"

I didn't let her finish. "I know where Xandra's jewelry box is."

"What?" she shrieked. "You found it?"

"Not exactly. What's your brother doing right now?"

"Big or little?"

"Big. Ronnie. Is he home?"

"Yeah, I think he's in the gara—"

"Can he come over right now and help me get the box?"

"Probably. I'm sure he'll help."

"Go get him. And hurry—we need to do this before my parents get home."

"What are we going—"

"Tell him to bring his rock-climbing gear. I'm in the backyard. Hurry!"

While I waited for Ronnie, I used a sharp rock to scratch a mark into the railing at the spot where the measuring tape ended. Suddenly I flinched. I'd heard something. Like a bush rustling, as if a small animal were climbing through it. Or a large human was hiding behind it.

My head whipped around and I looked into the corners of my backyard. It felt like someone was watching me. Moments later I knew I was right. Two round lenses were spying on me from behind the hedge in the neighbor's yard that backed to ours.

Binoculars. *With one brown eye looking through them?* As soon as I started to walk toward them to get a closer look, the lenses disappeared. Our neighbor's bushes were thick and I couldn't see anything except movement: a thin figure, sprinting away from his hiding place. Knowing he was busted. *Who was spying on me? Someone from Crew Gang? Who else could it be?*

The next-door neighbor had recommended Smack, and now one of his boys could be hiding in their yard. Were our neighbors plotting with them to find the hidden jewels? *Is that why those creeps were referred to us in the first place?* A chill crept up my spine.

No time to follow up on it now.

Ronnie's truck rumbled up the hill and stopped. I jogged back over to the fence and spotted his carrot-colored hair as he came through our side yard. He held a helmet and a pair of gloves and had a thick coil of rope over his shoulder. "Skylar!" Alexa shouted, running up to me. "I *knew* you could do it."

"So, little Skylar Robbins found the famous missing jewelry box?" Ronnie teased, dropping his rope on the grass.

"Not yet," I admitted, "but I think I know where it is. Thanks for coming over." I'd never been so glad to see anyone in my whole life.

"No problem." He scratched his head as he looked around our backyard. "So? Why'd you want me to bring my gear?"

"Because I'm pretty sure the box is twelve-and-a-half feet down there," I said, pointing over the railing. I lowered my voice. "By the way, did you see anyone run out of my neighbor's yard when you pulled up?"

He looked at me like I'd just guessed his birthday out of thin air. "Yeah. A skinny Hispanic guy. How'd you know?"

Ignado. Crew Gang was *watching me.* This chilled me for a second but I shook it off, hoping to hear a truck going down the hill like an animal crawling away with its tail between its legs. "Just a hunch. Hurry! We have jewels to find."

"Nobody told me to bring anything to dig with," he said, looking at Alexa like it was her fault. He attached a harness around his waist and thighs. Its buckles matched the one in the rusty metal box. "You think it's just gonna be sitting there on a rock or something?"

"I have no idea," I admitted. "But if I put the clues together right, it's five feet eight inches from the end of the railing and twelve-and-a-half feet down, marked by nasturtiums and mustard weeds. This is twelve-and-a-half feet of twine," I said, showing it to him. Then I tied one end to the railing at the spot I'd scratched with the rock, and flung the other end over the side and down into the canyon. "I think you're supposed to climb down the hillside, and when you get to the end of the twine you'll be in the right spot." I glanced into the neighbor's yard behind mine. Nothing moved. The street was quiet. *Too quiet.*

Alexa looked at me like I was a genius, and then turned toward her brother. "See? She knows where it is."

Ronnie tied his much thicker rope to the railing with a complicated knot, and attached the other end to his harness. Then he put on his helmet and a pair of thick gloves and jerked hard on the railing several times. "I want to be sure this thing can bear my weight," he explained. "I think we're good."

Alexa stood right next to me and we watched her brother throw his legs over the railing and then slowly climb down the hillside, gripping the rope tightly. The muscles in his freckled arms bulged, and his blue helmet looked smaller as he neared the spot where the twine ended. "No wonder you wanted Ronnie to come over, Skylar. You would have killed yourself trying to do this on your own."

"I know. I learned my lesson when I got stuck in the dumbwaiter."

"Hey!" Ronnie yelled. We leaned over the railing. He'd braced his feet against the hillside and was looking up at us.

"Did you find it?" I shouted.

"No, but I found something." Wrapping the rope tightly around his left hand, he thrashed his right hand around, batting thick mustard weeds and skinny nasturtium vines out of his way. "On the side of the hill right here, someone spray-painted a black *X* on a rock."

A huge smile spread across my face and I shouted, "Yes!" at the sky.

A minute later I heard the sound of a motorcycle ripping down our hill.

31
Xandra Collins's Jewels

barely made it through school on Friday, I was so nervous about what would happen at my house afterward. Not to mention that Ignado might have seen Robbie find the *X* on the hillside. If he did, then Crew Gang knew where Xandra's jewels were hidden too. And that meant they were planning something.

Alexa's mom dropped us off and we ran inside to get ready. "Your house looks great," Alexa said, following me through the entryway.

I looked around. Smack and his boys were nowhere in sight. "Thanks. Those creeps actually did a good job. Hopefully they won't show up any time soon."

Just then my mom rushed up to us. "Skylar," she said, "the news crew will be here any minute. Hurry up and change."

My dad had put gel in his hair and wore one of his best suits for the cameras. "The crane's already here, but I'm not sure about the rock-climber," he said, heading for the backyard.

I hated the formal dress my mom insisted I wear, and I begged her to let me choose another outfit. "But Mom, I solved the whole case and figured out where Xandra's jewelry box is buried. Shouldn't I be allowed to wear whatever I want on TV?" Suddenly this was just as important as whatever Smack and Ignado were up to.

"You're going to be interviewed, Skylar. Don't you want to look professional on the news? Everyone will be watching." I thought about this. "It's your first opportunity to introduce your detective agency. You don't want to look too casual."

She got me with that one. "You're right." As I ran upstairs to change I heard the doorbell ring. I put on the dress and brushed my hair, and by the time I flew back down the stairs the living room had started to fill up with people. Alexa sat on our couch with her hands folded in her lap, watching the camera crew set up with an excited smile on her face. I hurried across the room and sat right next to her. "I'm so nervous," I admitted. And it wasn't just because of the interview.

"Don't worry, Sky, you look beautiful and you'll kick butt. Like you always do," she said confidently. "Thanks for inviting me to come watch."

I turned to face her. "You sure you don't want to get up there with me?" I asked for the third time. "You were the one who figured out where the map started," I reminded her. "I wouldn't have found out where the jewelry box was buried without your help. And Ronnie's."

"No way." Alexa shrunk back into the couch. "I'm not making a fool of myself in front of any cameras." Then she paused, and a new expression bloomed on her face. "Actually," she said thoughtfully, "if there's something short you want me to read off a cue card I could probably handle it." She looked at me and opened her fingers, showing me the squishy ball in her left hand.

"I have no idea what they're going to ask me either. But if they call you up there I know you'll do great." We locked pinkies, and held on for a minute before we pulled them apart.

Another caravan of cars drove up our hill, fighting for spots along the side of our driveway. A blonde newswoman strolled into the room, picking out my mom and me. She walked up to us with her hand thrust forward and a big fake smile on her face. "I'm Trina Bradshaw from AFX," she announced. Trina had so much makeup on that she looked like a clown. "And you must be the little girl who solved the mystery."

I stared at her and didn't smile back. Since I was the one who had figured out where Xandra buried her jewels after adults had failed for three years, I didn't appreciate being called a little girl. Not to mention outsmarting a gang of construction workers who had monster tools and access to our entire house. Who were probably watching us at this very minute.

"I'm Skylar Robbins," I said, shaking her hand. "Of the Skylar Robbins Detective Agency."

"Oh aren't you cute?" she said, squeezing out another fake smile.

That did it. "I'm not a cute little girl. I'm a detective," I corrected her.

"Skylar," my mom warned. "Manners."

"That's perfectly OK." My dad stuck up for me. "She's right. Let them get it correct on the news." He nodded at me, and then walked back outside to supervise the television crew.

"Let's go see what's going on in the backyard," Alexa suggested.

"Good idea." I lowered my voice. "I have to talk to you."

We hurried outside and I filled her in as I walked.

"I think Smack's guys know I'm about to find the jewels. I spotted binoculars through the bushes when Robbie found the *X*. One of them was spying on me from the neighbor's yard."

"Seriously?" Alexa clamped her hand over her mouth and then took it away and stared right at me. "What do you want me to do?"

"Keep your eye on the street," I said, looking around. "And if you see any of the guys from the crew approach the house or if I give you the signal, call *9-1-1* and tell them there's an attempted robbery in progress. If Smack's guys don't try to take the jewels I'll tell the cops it was a false alarm."

"What's the signal?"

"9-1-1 in sign language." I touched my index finger to my thumb for *9*, then held up my first finger twice with my palm facing forward.

"Got it."

We walked farther into the yard and heard the crane driver, Bob Blare, arguing with my dad. He called the box at the top of the crane the "cherry picker." This was where a cameraman would sit and film the guy who dug into the mountainside. Bob wanted to get the cherry picker as close to the edge of the railing as possible, and my dad was afraid the crane would ruin our lawn. He was probably right, but once we had dug up Xandra Collins's jewels I didn't think losing a few blades of grass would really matter. I wished I were up in the cherry picker right now. I could see into our neighbor's yard and figure out if Sledge, Dusty, or Ignado were spying on us, waiting for me to find the jewelry box so they could rip it out of my hands.

Leaning to my right, I peeked through the side yard and tried to see past our house and out toward the street. Nothing suspicious seemed to be going on. Yet.

A balding guy with a big forehead rode over to the guardrail on a little tractor. He wore headphones and held a long pole with a microphone on the end of it, so I guessed he was the soundman. The mic was padded and he called the whole thing "the boom." My dad winced as his tractor left tracks in our new grass.

Two cute guys holding big white discs walked over to the metal railing next. The taller one had big eyes that were dark blue like mine. "You the girl who figured out the mystery?" He ran his hand casually through his slippery blond hair, and it fell back across his forehead.

"Yeah," I said, looking across the canyon. Then I smiled back at him. "I'm Skylar Robbins."

"I'm Mac. This is Johnny." Mac had nice teeth. Johnny shook my hand, and then held up his disc, tilting it at slightly different angles.

"What are those?" I asked.

"Photoflex Litediscs. To reflect the light onto you so we can get a good picture. Johnny, tilt yours back more. Stop right now. The light's perfect." Mac smiled at me. "You look great."

"Thanks," I said, trying not to blush. Mac was almost as cute as Dustin. But not quite.

The cameraman who was ready to film my interview was named Gordon. He was a thin Latino with twinkling brown eyes and a dimple. Trina Bradshaw rushed around frantically with Gordon at her side while the director bellowed orders at Tom and the guys with the Litediscs. Everyone wore headsets or wireless earpieces. Cell phones rang constantly and walkie-talkies chirped. I had never been so excited. I couldn't believe all of this was because of me!

My parents walked over to me and my dad squeezed my shoulder. He smiled, crinkling his eyes, and then looked at me tenderly. "I am so proud of you."

"And so am I," my mom said, smiling warmly at me.

"Thanks, Mom." I held out my arms for a hug. "I'm glad you suggested this dress," I whispered as she hugged me back.

"You figured out Xandra Collins's clues and used your brain to piece together a complicated puzzle. At the same time, you stood up to the bullies at your school, and never compromised your standards. You're the best daughter a parent could ask for."

"And you're a heck of a good detective," my dad added.

"That's for sure," my mom agreed, making me smile.

For a minute. I hoped they would still feel the same way if Crew Gang barged in and tried to steal the jewels, ruining everything. I imagined a violent fight: Smack and Ignado against Mac and Johnny, with my dad rushing in to break it up, all caught live on AFX for the evening news.

Trina Bradshaw hustled over. "We're almost ready to roll. Let's have you stand still so we can get a reading on the light." A guy with a fleshy pink face and a big belly came over and held a square light meter right in front of my chest, and then said something to Gordon who nodded from behind the camera. Mac and his buddy tweaked the position of the discs until the guy with the belly said, "That's it. Right there."

"Cell phones off, everybody," the director shouted.

My mom rushed over to me and pulled my long hair over my shoulders in front. "You look beautiful. Knock 'em dead." She walked away as Trina ran back up to me and Gordon started to count backward.

"And three, two, and-" He pointed at Trina.

"Today we join thirteen-year-old detective Skylar Robbins for the conclusion of a three-year-old mystery concerning the famous Xandra Collins jewelry collection," Trina Bradshaw gushed. "The excavation crew is ready and waiting for your instructions, Skylar." Trina was all teeth. "First, tell the world how you figured it out." She stuck the microphone right up to my mouth and I smelled her sour breath on its fuzzy black cover.

I cleared my throat and looked into the camera. My stomach had never been jumpier, and I almost would have given up the backwards dance to get out of doing this interview. But then I thought of the future of my detective agency and tried to ignore my nerves. "I just followed the clues that Xandra Collins left. One led to the next and it was really pretty simple. I couldn't believe in three years that her heirs never figured it out."

Trina smiled. "Witness the genius of Skylar Robbins! Walk us through your search for the jewels." Trina stuck her microphone back under my lips and waited for me to tell my story.

I looked back into the camera and took a deep breath. "After we moved in I noticed fingerprints on the windowsill in the room at the top of the turret, and they led me to an empty cupboard. I used the black light from my detective kit and found a note on the wall that Xandra Collins had written in invisible ink."

While I told my story, a photographer took shots of me while Gordon filmed my interview. Another cameraman sat in the crane and waited by the railing with the digger. A tan, muscular guy named Vladimir held a shovel and a bucket of tools. He had ragged light brown hair and crooked teeth, and he spoke with an accent. Talking into the microphone, I described the dumbwaiter and the pile of boxes, the footprint map, and the bird's nest clue.

"How did you end up at the edge of this cliff?" Trina Bradshaw asked. I waited while the crane made noise as the cherry picker carried the second cameraman out over the side of the mountain. When I turned to look at the camera, I thought I saw a round shape reflecting out of the next-door neighbor's bushes. Could it be Ignado's binoculars—spying on me again? As soon as I focused on it, the image vanished. I shook my head and stared, but there was nothing there. Maybe my imagination was playing tricks on me.

Forcing my eyes away, I tried not to stammer as I kept talking into the microphone. "I wouldn't have found the location without the help of my smart best friend, Alexa O'Reilly. I couldn't tell where the map started, but she looked into the backyard from a window in the turret and figured it out. Once she told me where to take the first step, I followed the footprints on the map, and they led me to a rusty metal box that was buried underneath the floor in the greenhouse." Looking over the heads of the film crew, I spotted Alexa standing with my mom. Her mouth dropped open and she clamped her hand over it when I said her name and gave her credit for helping me figure out where the jewels were buried.

I hoped when this interview was broadcast on TV that Dustin and Brendan would see it. Not to mention Emelyn Peters, Pat Whitehead, and all of the other kids who made fun of Alexa and didn't recognize how intelligent she really was. She promised to make sure her parents watched the news when my segment aired. Alexa's dad needed to hear how his daughter used her brains to help me solve the mystery. It was time he realized that Alexa was trying as hard as she could, and that she was smart, even though she had trouble reading and spelling.

"Inside the box there was a leaf, a buckle, a flower, a torn measuring tape, a packet of nasturtium seeds, and some twine," I continued.

"How did those clues lead you to this mountainside?" Trina smiled like an overgrown Barbie. I looked past the camera at Gordon and he gave me an encouraging nod.

"When I studied the clues in the box, I realized that the edges of the dead leaf had the same curvy shape as the leaves on the yellow-flowering weeds at the base of those boulders." I pointed down the hillside. "The dried-up flower had little dead petals on it that used to be mustard flowers. Inside the packet of nasturtium seeds there was a tiny gold key, and a note from Xandra Collins that said if I put the clues together and found the key I knew what it would unlock." Opening my hand, I revealed the little key. As Gordon zoomed in for a close-up, I heard a motorcycle climbing slowly up the hill.

So did everyone else. Trina dropped the microphone down by her side and waited for it to pass. It didn't. It stopped. My nightmare was about to come true—right while I was being filmed for the six o'clock news.

Alexa looked at me and I gave her a little nod, so scared I felt numb. She hurried into the side yard for a look at the street.

"And that's the key to Xandra Collins's jewelry box?" Trina continued, showing her teeth. She had no idea that a much more exciting event was unfolding just beyond the reach of her camera and microphone.

I gulped dryly and tried to work up some saliva so I could continue. "That's also when I realized what the twine was for. Her jewelry box is buried in the hillside," I said, wondering what was going on out front, and hoping Alexa was safe. "The torn measuring tape stops at five feet, eight inches. I tied a twelve-and-a-half-foot length of twine five feet, eight inches down the guardrail. Vladimir needs to climb down the side of the canyon right by the twine. At the very end of it he'll see a mustard plant and nasturtiums. There is a black *X* spray-painted on the rocks behind them. That's where he needs to dig into the hillside and look for the box."

Just then Alexa raced back into the yard, looking terrified. Pointing at the door, she flexed the muscles in both of her arms. I knew exactly what she meant: *Crew gang was back*. More determined than ever to snatch Xandra's jewels.

I signed, 9-1-1. Alexa nodded and ran into the house to call the police. *Sledge and Ignado could be on their way up to our front door right now. What if they had weapons?*

Once I found Xandra's jewelry box, would Smack wrestle it out of my hands at gunpoint and then zoom down the hill, carrying it away on his motorcycle?

Was this case about to end in a giant fail?

Trina wasn't about to let her prime-time piece get interrupted by some street noise. She grabbed my arm in an iron grip, grinning over her shoulder at the camera. "Show us where you found the next clue, Detective Skylar," she demanded, and we headed toward the edge of the cliff.

The cameraman moved over to the guardrail and the director yelled, "Action!" Tom bent over the side of the railing, aiming the boom down the steep canyon wall. Vladimir climbed into a harness that was attached to Tom's tractor with a thick cable and a huge metal clamp. He stepped over the guardrail and let himself slowly down the hillside, sliding one hand down the cable and holding a bucket of tools in his other, gritting his crooked teeth. When he got to the end of the twine he was in front of the patch of mustard plants and nasturtiums. He batted them around like Ronnie had until he spotted the X.

My eyes whipped back and forth between the camera and my house as I tried not to panic. Alexa ran back into the yard and fingerspelled something to me in sign language with her eyes open wide: C-O-P-S. She pointed her index fingers out, and then whipped them toward her body: COMING.

I heard a faint siren growing louder, and signed, GO SEE. Trina looked at the director and made a slashing motion across her throat. "Cut!" the director shouted.

Everyone stopped and waited for the siren to pass. Except it didn't. Alexa gaped at me as the siren made one last loud whoop and shut down. A cop car had just stopped right in front of our house.

The director's head whipped back and forth as he looked at me and then toward the side yard, as if he was hoping to see what was going on in the street. Trina glared at him as if having the camera on her was much more important than someone getting a ticket. His cheeks turned red as he yelled, "Roll film!" and Trina put the microphone up to my mouth.

"That's exactly where he needs to start digging," I said, looking at her and then into the camera, dying to know what was happening out front. Hoping the cops would catch Ignado and Smack before they barged into our yard and demanded that we hand over the jewels.

Vladimir spread his legs, pressing his shoes against the hillside. He grabbed a shovel and started to dig into the mountain. Gordon caught it all on film while everyone waited impatiently, some talking intensely on tiny cells. A minute later Vladimir waved his hand and called for everyone's attention. "Cell phones *off*," the director yelled again.

I stared at the gate. *What was happening in the street?!*

Reaching into one of the holes he had dug, Vladimir gently scraped the earth away using a small pick and a brush. The cameraman in the cherry picker zoomed in for a close-up. "I'm finding somezing," Vladimir announced.

A guy wearing a headset shouted, "I need better audio!" and Tom aimed the boom down the steep canyon wall. Looking toward the street, I tried not to panic. No one had burst through the side yard gate. Yet.

Trina stuck her stinky microphone into my face. "Well, Skylar, what do you think?"

I took a deep breath and swallowed my fear. "I think he's about to dig up Xandra Collins's jewels."

Moments later, Vladimir reached into the hole he had dug, and his hand came out holding a box wrapped in dirty plastic. After resting the box in the bucket with his tools, he climbed back up the hillside and vaulted over the guardrail. I knew he would let me open the box in front of the cameras, since this had been a part of the contract with AFX that my father had insisted on. Vladimir handed me Xandra Collins's jewelry box. "It is yours."

Trina looked at me triumphantly and said, "AFX is proud to capture this historic moment, LIVE!" I tore off the plastic bag. Curling designs were carved into rich, dark wood. There was a gold lock on the front of the box with a tiny keyhole. "Any last words from the Skylar Robbins Detective Agency?" she asked, and I nodded.

I cradled the heavy box in my hands. The microphone appeared in front of my mouth, and I smiled, holding up the key. "Case *closed*."

The director yelled, "Cut!" Trina Bradshaw motioned frantically, and Tom and Gordon hurried right over.

"We need a nice tight shot of her opening up the box," she snapped, using her raspy, everyday voice. Mac and his friend angled the Litediscs around until the guy holding the light meter in front of me nodded. AFX was ready to roll. "This is the end of a three-year search for Xandra Collins's jewels," Trina announced. "AFX is honored to be the first to capture this on film. Just moments ago, excavation expert Vladimir Azarov dug into this mountainside after following the clues that Skylar Robbins figured out, and he retrieved Xandra Collins's missing jewelry box. So if you are ready, Skylar, let's see what's inside!"

Then we heard a gunshot, and Alexa screamed.

32
The Skylar Robbins Detective Agency

"CUT!" the director yelled, as booted feet crunched across gravel and harsh shouts sounded from the street. Trina and the cameraman sprinted through the side yard to film the breaking story that was unfolding in front of my house.

My parents ran toward the side yard and I followed them, wobbling on my heels. We all rushed into the street and came to a screeching halt right behind Alexa. "Skylar!" she shouted, pointing.

A buff black cop had Smack pinned to the ground on his stomach—hog-tied with his feet and hands bound together up above his back. Smack's face was twisted in anger and fear. Alexa grabbed my arm and tried to catch her breath. "He had a gun! He was slipping through your neighbor's yard. Ready to run into yours. The guy with the bad eye had a knife in his hand! They tried to get away on their Harleys but the cops had them boxed in."

"Thanks for calling the police." I smiled, remembering Grandpa's words: *Criminals don't bother with houses in cul-de-sacs. They don't want to get trapped with no way out.* Unless there's a zillion dollar's worth of diamonds at stake, and they think they're smarter than everyone else. Smack hadn't thought he'd get trapped at the end of our street with no possible way to escape.

Alexa nodded. "The cops said a group called *The Wilkerson Boys, P.I.* were watching the house and called

223

them right before I did. Sounds like some of your secret agents?" I nodded. Alexa wiped sweat off her forehead and took another big breath. "So the police got here right when Smack was about to break in."

"Who fired the gun?" I asked.

"Smack. At one of the cops! He missed."

"So glad you all had my back," I said, grabbing Alexa in a quick hug.

Gordon and Trina ran out into the street, right behind my mom. I looked at Smack's motorcycle. A cop with a brown moustache had Ignado bent over it with his hands cuffed behind his back. Trina rushed up to the officer. "Please give us an update on this breaking news," she demanded, and then stuck her mike under his nose. He smelled it and winced. Alexa and I moved closer so we could hear him.

"Caught these two jokers just as they were about to run through the side yard. Both were armed and danger-ous. Stand back, please," he said, and then he read Ignado and Smack their Miranda rights. I knew them by heart, and mouthed them along with the cop with a little smile on my face. "You have the right to remain silent. Any-thing you say or do may be held against you in a court of law."

Moments later they were loaded into the back of a police van. My mom watched them sail down the hill with her mouth open. I followed her back into the yard with Alexa next to me, muttering, "Oh my God, did you see that, Skylar? Oh my God."

"I knew it," I said, trying not to look at my mom.

Too late. She grabbed my arm and spun me around

so I was facing her. "What do you mean, you knew it? What do you know about this, Skylar?"

"Smack and his gang. I knew they were up to no good," I finally admitted, taking a deep breath and blowing it out.

"How did you know, and why didn't you say something?" My mom dragged her hands through her hair and looked like she wanted to strangle me.

Gulp. "I didn't have any proof, and they hadn't really done anything yet."

Except threaten me with a dead rodent. But I knew they were after Xandra's jewelry box too. And I wasn't going to let them win.

"So I had to let the cops catch them in the act. And I just did," I said, waiting nervously for my mom's reply.

She looked at me angrily, and then she relaxed a little and sighed. "OK. I am glad you let the police handle it," she said. "But you should have told us that you suspected those men were up to no good much earlier."

"I know, Mom. And I'm sorry." This time I really did mean it. I had a feeling some punishment might be in my immediate future. And I probably deserved every bit of it. I planned to tell her all of the details later and accept the consequences. "And I think the neighbors," I lowered my voice and pointed with my eyes to the house behind the hedges, "might have been in on it."

"*What? Why?*"

"Because they recommended them for one, and I think Ignado has been spying on me from behind their bushes."

She stared at the tall shrubs separating our yards as

if someone might pop out of them at any second. They remained still. My mom looked like she was calculating something. "Well, we can ask the police to investigate that, but that's some pretty flimsy evidence."

I nodded, "You're right. I'm just glad those crooks got busted. And best of all, I found Xandra's jewels!" Her eyes softened and she folded me into a hug. Then she smiled. It was pretty exciting!

"OK, chop chop, people," Trina called, snapping her fingers. Back to business.

I really wanted to open Xandra's jewelry box in private, but with the cameras rolling, I knew I didn't have a choice. The street was quiet. The cops and Crew Gang were gone. There was nothing standing between Xandra's fortune and me. My detective agency was about to explode, right on the evening news.

I walked back to where I had stood before, and Mac moved the Litedisc around until Gordon nodded. The director shouted, "Action!" And I slid the little gold key into the lock.

With shaking fingers I turned the key, unhooked the catch, and slowly pried the lid open.

"*Wow*," I breathed. Xandra's jewels were just as incredible as Ms. Knight said they would be. A buzz spread through the crowd as more people leaned in to get a closer look at the diamonds. I heard my mom gasp when she finally saw the jewelry.

The huge diamond necklace that Xandra Collins wore in the photograph glittered in the sunshine. The large stones were dazzling in their brilliance; rainbows of sunlight reflected off them and shot out at every angle.

Beside the necklace a diamond bracelet shimmered on red velvet, just as sparkling and impressive. There were matching diamond earrings, and several delicate bracelets and rings.

Scattered around and underneath the diamonds were a black-pearl brooch, a gorgeous pin decorated with rubies and amethysts, an emerald bracelet, and rings covered in shining stones of different colors. One had a diamond on it the size of a large grape. I picked up a charm bracelet with glimmering jewels attached, and saw a set of bangles decorated with precious gems underneath it. There were gold chains with jeweled pendants, and an awesome tennis bracelet with large square diamonds all around it.

There was a shallow drawer below the main box that I saved to open later, in private. I tried to keep my hand in front of it so Trina wouldn't force me to open it on national TV. She leaned toward me. "Look at these jewels! I understand that Xandra Collins left a note that said whoever is smart enough and brave enough to follow her clues and figure out where the jewelry box was hidden would inherit her fortune in diamonds, and that, my friend, is *you*. Tell the world how you feel." She pointed the microphone at my mouth.

My stomach felt like it had a football game raging inside it, but I tried to ignore the feeling. This was my chance to advertise my detective agency, and I was going to make the most of it. I looked right into the camera, took a deep breath, and cleared my throat. "I am happy to announce that the Skylar Robbins Detective Agency has solved its first big case. And I look forward to my next one."

The director shouted, "Cut!"

Gordon ran up to Trina and said something to her while I looked through the jewels with my parents by my side.

I heard Trina say, "Great idea," and then she rushed up to me. "Skylar, we'd like to get a shot of you wearing the big diamond necklace, Sweetie, OK?" I looked at my mom and she nodded. My dad held the jewelry box to keep it safe and my mom picked up the heavy diamond necklace and fastened it around my neck. Her fingers felt clammy against my hot skin. Boy was I glad she had made me put on a nice dress, because now I knew what "dripping in diamonds" meant. If I had to wear Xandra's diamond necklace with the rhinestone top I'd picked out I would have been dripping in stupid.

Then Gordon called for our attention. "Let's have your parents stand on either side of you," he suggested. "Skylar, you hold the jewelry box in front of you." He gestured at my parents. "Move in closer behind Skylar please. Tighter," he said, and my mom and dad shuffled in until they were standing right next to each other behind me. Gordon picked up an expensive-looking camera with a square flashbulb attached to the top of it. He took lots of pictures of me holding the box and wearing the diamond necklace, and then took shots of the cherry picker and of Vladimir holding the coiled rope and his big pick.

Gordon finally photographed our guardrail and the canyon, and then everyone packed up and left as quickly as they had come. I walked inside wearing the heavy necklace around my neck and a huge smile on my face.

Smack and his gang were on their way to jail and I had found the hidden jewels. Another case *closed*. If Grandpa had still been alive, I know exactly what he would have said, and I heard it in my mind and felt it in my heart.

"I'm *proud* of you."

33
Fame

Alexa called me Sunday night. I answered my cell and heard her screaming my name on the other end of the line. "Skylar Robbins you're on the news, right now! You're about to say my name! Turn on channel—"

"I'm watching it! Call you back." My parents and I were so excited that we were all watching television standing up. Trina Bradshaw looked much prettier on TV than she did in person.

"Honey, you look gorgeous," my mom said, touching my hair. "You are one super daughter. I guess this time taking some risks paid off," she admitted, looking at my dad. Working with Alexa to get the thieves arrested and then locating a fortune in diamonds had taken her mind off the danger I'd put myself in. For now.

My dad smiled at her and then gave us a group hug. "Detective Supermodel," he complimented me, pointing at the television. I looked way different on TV than I do in the mirror, that's for sure. I wondered how many people I knew were watching my interview. The next morning I found out.

By the time I got to school Monday I was famous. Not only had they all seen me on the news, but a picture of me wearing the huge diamond necklace already had hundreds of retweets. I was holding the jewelry box, standing in front of my parents who were smiling like crazy. A video of me opening the box and showing the jewels had gone viral. I walked up to English class with a crowd of kids around me, asking questions so fast I didn't have time to answer.

"When did you start your own detective agency?"

"You're rich now, right?" Jamal smiled.

"Did Alexa really help you find the jewelry box?" Sharon wondered.

"Definitely," I answered. "I couldn't have done it without her."

"I didn't know you were that smart. You're really a detective?" someone asked.

"What are you going to do with the jewels?"

Dustin looked at me. "Where are they now?"

I thought I'd answer his question. "My dad put them in a safe until I figure out if I want to sell them or what." I sat in my seat and the others crowded around me like I was a celebrity. I didn't like it, and wondered why people try to get famous. It made me feel very uncomfortable. But there was one thing I was thankful for: Crew Gang was going to jail for attempted robbery, weapons charges, and assaulting an officer, so I didn't have to worry about them anymore.

"I'm so proud of you," Alexa said, when we met at our locker at the break. "I *knew* you'd figure it out. Thanks for calling me your smart best friend on TV," she said, and her eyes misted up.

"You *are* my smart best friend."

By lunchtime my fame had faded and everybody was tired of the subject of Xandra Collins's jewels. Something more important was on everyone's minds. The backwards dance was Friday night! Alexa and I sat down at an empty table and started eating our sandwiches.

"So is Brendan picking you up or meeting you there?"

She put her hand over her mouth to hide the food in her smile. "He said he'd meet me there. What about Dustin?"

"We haven't talked about it since he'd told me he'd go, but I'll ask him to meet me there too so you and I can get ready together. Then maybe your mom can take us there and my mom can bring us home or something." That was the best idea I'd had yet. I'd been panicking thinking about Dustin's parents picking me up on our first date and trying to make conversation with him in the backseat of their car.

I finished my sandwich and wiped my mouth, then threw away my paper bag and sat back down. Taking my little makeup mirror out of my purse, I checked my teeth and popped a breath mint. My nerves felt jumpy as I thought about the dance.

34
Friday Night

Before we knew it, Friday night had arrived. Alexa came over for dinner, and after forcing down some meatloaf we ran up the stairs to my room to get ready. I took the first shower and put on plenty of deodorant and lots of lotion.

"Want to see my dress?" Alexa asked. I nodded and she pulled a thin plastic sheet off of the hanger, showing me an emerald green dress with a tropical flower print.

"That's *so* cute. My mom bought me a new outfit too." I took the dress out of my closet and pulled it down over my head. It was kind of tight fitting and came down to just above my knees, and it was the same deep blue as the ocean on a really sunny day.

"It matches your eyes perfectly," Alexa said.

I carefully put on my first pair of nylons, hoping I wouldn't get a run in them. Then I stepped into a new pair of shoes and walked awkwardly around my room, trying to break them in a little. "Hope I don't stumble on the dance floor and make a fool of myself in front of Dustin."

"You won't."

"Do you think I'll be taller than him in these heels?"

Alexa looked at the top of my head seriously. "No. I think you'll be just the same height."

"Good. As long as I'm not taller. And guess what? My dad locked most of Xandra's jewels in his safe, but I was allowed to pick out a couple of her smaller pieces.

My mom let me wear one of Xandra's rings tonight since it's a special occasion. Follow me." We went upstairs into my office. "Close your eyes," I said, pulling out the center drawer of my desk. Reaching behind it, I slid the panel sideways, revealing the secret compartment. I reached past Grandpa's badge and pulled out a tiny velvet box.

Lifting the lid, I took out the sparkling sapphire ring. It wasn't actually so little after all, and it matched the blue of my dress perfectly. I slipped it onto my finger and hid something else in my other hand. "Look."

Alexa opened her eyes. "That's beautiful," she breathed, gazing at my ring.

"I have a surprise for you too," I said, my fingers curling around a delicate gold bracelet. "Hold out your hand." She opened her palm and I dropped the gift into it. "This is for you."

In between two lengths of gold chain there was a small emerald imbedded in a gold heart. "Oh my God," Alexa said, sucking in her breath. "To wear to the dance, or for keeps?"

"For keeps. My parents said I could give you something for helping me find the jewels. I thought you'd like this bracelet."

"I *love* it." Alexa hugged me, and then I hooked the clasp while she stared at the bracelet. Then she looked up at me. "You would have figured out where the map started without me, Skylar."

"Maybe. But maybe not. The important thing is, you figured out where it started and I found the jewels because you helped." I looked at my desk clock. "Hey, we better finish getting ready. It's almost time to leave."

We walked carefully to the bathroom in our heels and took turns brushing on a little eye shadow.

"Want some perfume?" Alexa asked. "It's new. Smell." She held it out and I breathed in the scent of fresh flowers.

"Yum. That smells great," I said, dabbing some of her perfume on my neck. Then we both bent forward and looked into the mirror. Alexa put on lip gloss, and I took out a light pink Ultrashine Lipslick and smoothed the glistening cream over my lips. When we were finally ready to go, we went back to my bedroom and stood close together. I held my cell phone in front of us, took our picture, and posted it on Instagram and Facebook. Then we left the house to go on our very first date.

Fifteen minutes later we climbed out of my mom's car and walked across the campus toward the gymnasium where the dance was being held. "School looks so different at night," Alexa said. Grass crunched beneath our shoes as we crossed the dark lawn, heading toward the lunch area.

"I know. It's kind of creepy." Our heels clacked on the cement hallways and echoed. It sounded menacing. I wondered if someone was following us.

"Let's hurry," Alexa said, and we walked faster. Echoed louder. Light from a dim bulb cast long shadows under the tables as we passed the cafeteria.

Suddenly someone hissed at us from around the corner of the building. "Hey, *Snitch*." I recognized that harsh, ugly twang.

Oh *no*. Alexa and I looked at each other and hobbled

faster in our new heels.

"Hey, *losers*," a second voice growled.

"Come on," Alexa said, grabbing my arm.

"I can't run in these shoes!" *Please don't let anything ruin my date with Dustin.*

Emelyn Peters and Pat Whitehead stepped out from behind the wall. They stood in front of us under a circle of weak yellow light with their arms folded, blocking our path to the gym. "What do you want?" I hoped they didn't notice my voice was quivering.

Emelyn leaned into me. "I want you to go *home* because I'm going to the dance with Dustin," she threatened. "Or you're dead meat."

"You aren't allowed to be here," Alexa said, sticking up for me.

"Shut up," Pat said, giving Alexa an aggressive little push in the chest. My BFF staggered backward, awkward in her new heels.

"I know what else I want." Emelyn was right up in my face. Her breath smelled like rotten garbage. "I'll take that ring you're wearing." She laughed a nasty, high-pitched giggle and grabbed my hand, trying to wrestle Xandra's sapphire ring off my finger. "I saw you on TV, you wannabe detective. You got a whole jewelry box. You won't miss this little ring, now will you?" She twisted my ring angrily, but I made a fist so she couldn't get it off my finger. "I'll end up taking the rest of your jewelry collection too."

"Oh no you won't," I said furiously. "It's locked up, like you're about to be."

Emelyn hadn't noticed the security guard walking

up behind her until it was too late. "Problem ladies?" he asked. She turned around to run and he caught her by the wrist. Pat stood there stunned, too surprised to move.

"Yes, Sir," I said. "Emelyn Peters just told me that I was 'dead meat' if I didn't let her go to the dance with my date, and then she tried to steal my ring."

"Plus she's not even allowed on campus except for classes," Alexa said. "She was caught stealing and they're the ones who vandalized the snack machine."

"You're such liars," Emelyn sneered.

"They're both full of it," Pat agreed.

"Oh we're not lying," I replied. In one smooth motion I fished my cell phone out of my purse, touched the screen twice, and showed it to the guard. His eyes widened as he watched Pat and Bart rock the vending machine back and forth until snacks started to fall off their hooks. My video ended when Emelyn stuffed the treats into her backpack and then looked over her shoulder, right into the camera, guilty as charged.

"Let's go, Miss Peters," the guard said. Emelyn struggled for a minute, trying to free her arm, but he just gripped it tighter. "You too," he barked at Pat.

"Why me?" Pat whined.

"Probably because you helped break the vending machine," I said.

"Oh *right*, Skylar." Pat squinted at me with her mouth open. "That isn't even me on your stupid phone."

"Sure looked like you to me," the guard said.

"It's not," she lied.

"Pat Whitehead's peacock's eye fingerprints are all over the left side of the vending machine, and Principal

Martinez has a copy of them on file if you need more proof," I told him. Now Pat's mouth fell open for real. "Ready Alexa?" We headed for the gym as the guard led Emelyn and Pat away.

"Hey, I hear music," Alexa said, cocking her head.

"Let's hurry. The dance is starting!" I grabbed Alexa's arm, and we hurried through the shadows toward the pulsing lights behind the gymnasium door.

35
The Backwards Dance

uffy cotton clouds hung from the ceiling, and a shiny sliver of glitter-covered moon winked at us from a far corner. Colored spotlights lit up a sparkling rainbow, and a disco ball swirled, reflecting dots of light that danced around the gym. Alexa and I walked around slowly, looking for Brendan and Dustin. "They know we're coming together, right?" I asked.

We crossed the slippery wood floor in our new heels and Alexa grabbed my arm so she wouldn't fall. "Yes. Brendan said they were coming together too, so hopefully they're both here." The band took the stage and played the first melodic chords in the dark. Then cymbals crashed, guitars wailed, and a spotlight shined on the stage, lighting up our side of the room. I saw Brendan and Dustin standing by the wall and cupped Alexa's ear. "There they are."

"Let's go freshen up our lip gloss before they see us!"

We ran into the crowded bathroom and wiggled between the girls and up to the mirror. I pulled out my new pink Lipslick. "Want some?" I asked Alexa, but she shook her head and put on some pale peach lip gloss that looked great against her light skin.

Sharon Greenburg was brushing her frizzy hair in front of the mirror but she stopped and turned to us when we walked in. "Hi, Skylar. Hey, Alexa."

"Hi, Sharon," I said.

"I got my pen back." Sharon tried to smile, but she

looked sad. "I got Emelyn in lots of trouble."

"You did the right thing," Alexa told her.

"Yeah, but I lost my best friend." Sharon searched our eyes.

"Anyone who steals from you isn't your friend," I said. "You can do better than Emelyn, Sharon."

Sharon stared at me through her thick glasses and finally nodded. "Thanks, Skylar," she said, and we walked out into the dark gym together.

Brendan and Dustin weren't standing where we last saw them, so we wandered over to the punch table and got cups. Mark Oglethorpe walked up to us and asked Sharon to dance. I'd never seen a bigger smile.

All of a sudden I felt a hand on my shoulder. I turned around and there they were. "Hi, Skylar," Dustin said. He looked a little nervous, like he couldn't decide what to say. Dustin took a look around the dark room, and then smiled shyly at me. "You look really nice tonight."

My heart thudded and I felt my cheeks flush. "Thanks. So do you," I answered, looking at his black button-up shirt and new jeans.

Brendan said something to Alexa right as the band started a new song. She leaned into him and a little punch dribbled out of her glass and splashed on the floor. I was embarrassed for her until Brendan pointed at the spill and said something that made Alexa laugh.

Dustin asked a question that I didn't hear and I set my glass down on the table so I wouldn't spill punch on him. He put his hand on my shoulder and repeated, "Want to dance?"

The band started a fast song and I knew if I tried to

dance to it I'd look like a total dork. Kids started bouncing around near us. I leaned in and cupped Dustin's ear, smelling the clean scent of his shampoo. "We just got here, can we wait a little bit?" I asked, and he nodded and smiled. I think he was relieved.

"Your interview on the news was great," he said. "Can't believe you figured out what all those clues meant."

"Well, I had help."

"Still. That was pretty awesome."

Colored spotlights circled around the floor. I waited for our area to light up and then showed him my ring. "This is from the jewelry box."

He glanced at it and smiled. Then he looked me in the eye. "Nice." A shiver ran down my spine as I stared back at him in the sparkling lights thrown off by the disco ball.

The band started to play a slow song and Dustin held out his hand. I hoped mine wasn't sweaty. I looked over at Alexa and she grinned at me. She was still joking around with Brendan and I could tell they weren't ready to dance yet, so I handed her my purse to hold, then let Dustin lead me onto the dance floor.

We turned toward each other with couples moving all around us. Dustin opened his arms and looked at me with a question in his eyes. I stepped forward and put my arms around his neck, and our bodies slowly pressed together. Between the mirror ball's spinning lights and the feeling of leaning against Dustin Coles, I felt deliciously dizzy.

Remembering the security guard leading Pat and Emelyn off campus, I was so glad I had Dustin to myself, and that I was safe and sound in his arms for the rest of the dance.

Unfortunately, almost all of the band's songs were fast ones, and I only got to slow-dance with Dustin twice. On the second slow song I rested my head on his shoulder. His hair smelled awesome and I think he'd even put on a little cologne for me. We weren't really dancing, just kind of swaying back and forth to the music. I knew I'd never forget the feeling of his arms around my waist, pulling me against his body. It felt so good I wished the song would never end.

Before we knew it the band announced their last song, which was a fast one, and then the lights came up and the chaperones announced that the dance was over. Alexa and I walked toward the door, and Brendan and Dustin followed us out into the dark night.

I had a sudden fear that Emelyn would be out there waiting for us with Pat, but we got to the sidewalk without any drama. Rows of cars with parents in them were double-parked up and down the street, so I felt pretty safe. Alexa's mom wasn't there yet, but Dustin's brother was, and we spotted the black Porsche right away. "I gotta go, Skylar, see you Monday."

"See you Monday." I thought he would just walk away, but then he turned around and my heart stopped. He walked up to me and it felt like I was watching him in slow motion. I saw Alexa out of the corner of my eye and her jaw dropped open. My mouth went dry and I was so glad I had popped a breath mint before the end of the dance.

Was Dustin about to kiss me? Was my first real kiss about to happen on the sidewalk in front of a traffic jam?

I looked at his cute face and waited for him to make the next move with my heart pounding.

Dustin reached up and touched my hair, then pulled my face gently toward his. He closed his eyes and his smile disappeared. I put one hand on his chest and the other on his shoulder. Dustin wrapped his arm around my back and stepped a little closer to me. I smelled the fresh scent of his hair. Then he leaned in and pressed his lips softly against mine. My first kiss made me feel like I was floating and falling all at the same time. Moments later he pulled back and I could breathe again.

"Bye, Skylar," he whispered into my ear. He turned away and then he was gone, leaving me tingling on the sidewalk waiting for my ride.

36
Skylar Robbins: Teen Detective

Saturday morning I woke up in a sleeping bag in Alexa's room with a smile on my face. The backwards dance had been the most exciting night of my whole life, and I had the rest of the semester left to enjoy with Dustin Coles in two of my classes. Best of all, now I knew for sure that he liked me.

I turned over and looked at Alexa as she sat up and yawned. "The dance was great, wasn't it?" I asked her, anxious to talk about Dustin.

"It was so fun."

"Do you think Brendan likes you?" I sat up and hugged my knees, pushing messy hair over my shoulders.

"Not as much as Dustin obviously likes you," she said, grinning at me. I could tell she wasn't jealous and I was glad.

"How do you know he likes me?" I couldn't wipe the smile off my face.

"I saw him kiss you when we were standing on the sidewalk," Alexa said, pointing at me.

"It was like for two seconds," I protested. "That doesn't necessarily—"

Alexa cut me off. "It sure does. It means *he likes you*!" she argued, and I got the tingling feeling back.

Alexa's mom drove me home after breakfast. The sunshine sparkling on the ocean reminded me of the disco ball throwing off dots of light at the dance. I smiled as we passed the pier. The big Ferris wheel spun slowly around and I imagined the excited laughter of the kids who were riding it. It was a beautiful day and the parking lot was full. Soon we were headed up the steep wooded hill toward my house. I didn't know how I'd be able to get through the weekend waiting for Monday when I'd see Dustin again.

After I unpacked my overnight case, I realized that I felt a little disappointed. The dance was over and so was the mystery of the hidden jewels. Our neighbors had been questioned and cleared of any involvement with the attempted robbery. I didn't have a new case to investigate, and it would be a long time before I was old enough to fly to foreign countries doing undercover detective work.

I walked downstairs looking for my dad, and found him puttering in his gadget room. "Hi, Dad."

"Hi, Skylar." He turned away from a table full of treasures and looked at me. "How was the dance?"

"Excellent." I knew I had a goofy look on my face from the way my dad smiled at me.

"Have a nice time with your date?" Then he actually winked.

"Yeah I did. But I wanted to ask you something."

He looked at me seriously. "Yes?"

"After you put Xandra Collins's jewels in the safe, what happened to the jewelry box? There was a little drawer in the bottom that I wanted to look in." I shifted my weight from one foot to the other. Thinking about the dance had distracted me, and I had forgotten to see what was in there. I hoped my dad had kept the empty jewelry box!

He smiled and walked over to the train table, taking Xandra's box out from a deep drawer underneath it. "Here you go. It's yours, just like her jewels. Don't forget, we need to make a decision about them."

As part of a follow-up story for AFX, Trina Bradshaw and her investigative reporters located a copy of Xandra Collins's mysterious note, willing her jewelry to the person who found it. A handwriting expert confirmed that it came from Xandra, my dad had it notarized, and the jewels were really mine. I knew we would end up selling most of the jewelry and investing the money in stocks and bonds. My dad said the biggest diamond necklace would pay for my college education. That thing was huge.

My life was definitely changed forever. After I turned eighteen I could control my own money and basically afford to buy anything I wanted. My mom was already lecturing me on the dangers of careless spending and encouraging me to keep the money invested until after I finished college. I also planned to donate some money to charity. Maybe one that worked on a cure for dyslexia.

"Thanks, Dad," I said, looking at the dirty jewelry box. "First thing I think I'll do is clean this thing up." I ran up the stairs to my room and climbed the spiral stairs to my office. The hand-lettered sign on my door looked tacky. I could afford to get a real sign made now.

I sat at my desk, put the jewelry box down, and opened the lid. It was empty. I felt the soft red velvet in the bottom of the box, thinking about Xandra Collins. Pulling her picture out of my clue box, I stared at her beautiful face, her tilting eyes, and her mischievous smile. I wondered for the hundredth time what had happened to her.

What an amazingly cool thing to do, hiding her jewelry box and leaving clues for someone to find, and then letting that person keep the jewelry. I remembered the note written on the inside of the packet of seeds: *At the end of the rope you will find the beginning of new adventure.* Could it top the adventure I'd just had? Enlisting the help of a smart group of secret agents, putting my life in danger, taking risks and challenging my BFF while she pushed me right back, stretching my detective skills to new limits?

I had accomplished a lot. And I was proud of myself. I couldn't wait for my next adventure to begin. Taking a look around my cozy office, I savored this moment, knowing that there might be another secret waiting for me. I slowly slid open the narrow drawer in the bottom of the jewelry box. It was empty.

But when I ran my fingertips over the soft velvet, I felt a long flat bump underneath. I took out my magnifying glass and examined the edge of the drawer until I found a little slit on one side where the red velvet was stapled to the wood. Wiggling my pinky in between the material and the wood, I loosened the fabric until I'd made a two-inch gap.

I reached inside, touched the flat bump, and felt a folded piece of paper. I pulled it out and carefully opened it.

Congratulations. You were smart and brave enough to follow my clues and locate my jewelry box. If you found it in the mountainside, I have either been kidnapped, killed, or I have been forced to go into hiding. Now the jewels are yours, and I need your help.

Find out who has been stalking me and help me bring them to justice!

You will find clues that will help your search when you locate my hidden diary.

GL URMW NB WR@+B BLF NFHG TL Y@XP GL GS% SRWW%M U&LL+

Another secret code! What did it mean? Where did I start? The first thing I needed to do was to find the entrance to the secret staircase and get back to the hidden floor. I couldn't wait to ask Alexa to be my permanent assistant detective so we could figure out more clues together. The excitement I'd felt while I was trying to solve the mystery of Xandra Collins's hidden jewelry box was back.

I slipped the ring off my finger and set it down on the red velvet. I wasn't selling this piece of Xandra Collins's jewelry. No way. The sapphire ring was proof that the Skylar Robbins Detective Agency had solved its first big case.

I unlocked my clue box and tucked in the coded note next to the labeled sets of fingerprints, my picture of Xandra Collins, the symbol on the tattered yellow paper, the photocopied footprint map, the nasturtium seed packet, and the original bird's nest papers. I stashed the clue box in my bottom desk drawer, then slid the panel behind the main drawer sideways and opened the secret compartment.

I took out the flat white box and opened it. Running my fingers over the shiny gold badge, I thought about my grandfather and knew I would have made him proud. I smiled as I read: *Detective Robbins.* "That's me too," I whispered.

Then I sat at my desk with my chin in my hands, looking out the window across the canyon and thinking.

If I figured out where Xandra Collins had hidden her jewelry box, surely I could decode her message and find her diary. Could the clues inside it help me figure out who had been stalking Xandra and what had happened to her? Could I solve this new mystery without putting myself in danger? I was itching to try to crack that code.

I turned on my iPad and opened my note-taking app. I was definitely ready for a new adventure. My fingers tingled with excitement as I named the entry to record my next case:

The Mystery of the Missing Heiress.

THE END

Made in the USA
San Bernardino, CA
04 December 2015